Touching Other Lives

Volume 3
Episodes 15-21

by

Margaret Gregory

Touching Other Lives

Volume 3
Episode List

Episode 15	Double Crossing	1
Episode 16	Where is Abbie?	28
Episode 17	Setting a Trap	56
Episode 18	Counter Trap	82
Episode 19	Martin's Troubles	109
Episode 20	Finding facts	139
Episode 21	Adding Pieces Together	170

Episode 15

Double Crossing

Chapter 1

Abbie had been glad to have slept on the bus coming down from NSW. Her mother had only waited long enough to be sure the hotel staff person had brought all their luggage up before deciding she really needed her hair done. "You need a haircut too," she decided, "and the colour redone."

"Really?" Abbie exclaimed in delight. Mostly her mother did the colour for her hair. Having it done by a professional would be great. She had stopped wondering why she had to have blond hair, instead of brown, but it had always been that way, and she liked being blond.

"When can we do it?"

"I'll just ring down to find out. This evening, I hope. They are open until late."

Her mother must have noticed that detail as soon as they had arrived. It seemed they were in luck. They still had appointments available. It would be a lot more interesting than watching old movies like on the bus.

Naturally, her mother was organised first. Abbie was asked to wait. Her hair professional would be with her soon. After five minutes, she was getting bored. She wanted to be back home, where she had stuff to do. How come her father had made them stay in the hotel? Her mother seemed to love the idea, but the room seemed to be a luxuriously stultifying cage. All the other shops except the café were shut for the night.

Her hand reached for her phone, and she idly tried to

connect her new phone to the hotel wi-fi. Then she considered ringing someone – but who? She hadn't called anyone with it yet.

Really, there were only two numbers she even considered, because both were people outside her usual life. She'd liked Wanda, when they'd worked on the garden. Hadn't been too sure of Robbo, so she tried Wanda's number. It was off. She decided to see how Robbo sounded on the phone.

"Is that Robbo?" she asked when the voice just said, "Hi, what do you want?"

"Yeah."

"It's Abbie."

"Abbie? Well, how are you, little Sis? What's up?"

"Not much," Abbie said. "Just wanted to know if you meant what you said. That I could stay with you?"

"Of course. What's happened?"

"I'm just tired of being pushed around like a chess piece."

"Where's he got you now?"

"I'm in Melbourne, but he dragged us up to some hick place in NSW then all of a sudden said we had to come back by bus and stay at a hotel. He's got mum acting as jailer. He doesn't want us at home."

"Well, he did have a bunch of really odd visitors last night," Robbo told her.

"He has clients visit sometimes," Abbie returned.

"Nah, these didn't look like sheep waiting to be fleeced. They looked dangerous."

"He might be in trouble?"

"If he is, he deserves it," Robbo said derisively. "He didn't call the police though. He got visited later, but they were using some ruse to go in and check him out. Something about there being an escaped criminal in the area. I had to stop watching. The police were as thick as fleas on a stray mutt."

Abbie began to have conflicting thoughts. Maybe her dad wanted them to stay away because of that?

"Hey, sis? I can pick you up if you want."

"I...I'll let you know. I'm out with mum right now. I would need to go back to our room to get stuff."

"Where are you staying?"

"At the Crown Towers," Abbie admitted. "It's posh, but it's suffocating. Ah, I have to go, okay?"

Abbie allowed the young woman to lead her to a chair to get her hair washed. She had not had half as much luxury for a mere haircut, ever. She might as well enjoy it. Besides, it would give her a chance to think.

Her conscience began to bother her. Perhaps she shouldn't have told Robbo so much. Yet his voice had sounded welcoming. Maybe when they met at the park, he'd been angry at her father – their father. What if her father was right, and they weren't his kids? If her father really was worried about her and mum. Was she being unreasonable?

Robbo definitely had a down on her father, and if they were his kids and he'd rejected them, she didn't blame them for hating him. Their mother and her father might have argued and all, and got divorced, like Jackie's parents had. Or, they could be lying, and she had no way to be sure.

Then another niggling voice in her head recalled that Annie had thought her dad a conman. And her sort of relatives, who knew him when he and her mum had met, thought him a slick talking shyster. Another idea followed. He had Gabrielle Hartley's birth certificate. What was that about? She hadn't mentioned that to anyone. Particularly not Gail and the others. They'd been snickering about Annie's interest in old Mad Maude Hartley. Was her father really going to pretend she was that woman's daughter? Was she in fact? Oh, how Gail would react to that! She didn't want anything to do with a mad woman, inheritance or no. Her dad was well off, she didn't need...no, he didn't need to grab some poor old woman's inheritance...like he'd done to Robbo's mum. Odds on, her dad would have control of any money she got, and that would be all she saw of it. And if it was a blatant scam, would she get blamed for it too?

She let the chatter of the hairstylist distract her for a bit. Something said prompted the idea of trying to call Wanda again, for an outside, unbiased view. Probably not at this late hour though. Wanda's phone might have needed charging.

Abbie was finished long before her mother would be. So she decided to go and ask, "Can I go across the way for a milkshake from the café?"

Victoria, sitting under a hair heater thing, only said, "Come right back, okay?"

"Sure, Mum." Abbie wondered what her mother could do if she didn't.

Her mother was enjoying herself too much to care. She was even having her nails done while the hair treatment was curing. Anyway, what was wrong with her going there by herself? She wasn't a child. She was nearly an adult.

She felt grown up as she ordered a milkshake and a slice of lemon cheesecake, and selected a stool near the window to have it. There she could watch the few people still moving about the hotel lobby, and use her phone. She tried the number for Wanda but it rang out again and went to the generic answering service.

"Hi, it's Abbie. Just thought I'd see how you were."

So much for help from her, Abbie thought, dismissively. Her drink arrived, and she kept thinking until it was gone. She still wasn't too sure about Robbo and Thea, and if Wanda didn't call back, all she could do was go back to her mum. Even in her own mind, she didn't want to remember when she had tried to go off with Adam. That was too humiliating. But if anything, Wanda was right. If she didn't feel comfortable doing something, she shouldn't. Well, she didn't like the idea of pretending to be someone she wasn't.

Victoria Carson called room service and ordered a fancy meal. When it came, the waiter might have been a non-entity as far as she was concerned. She was playing the 'very rich lady' and not even looking at the man as she gave him direction for where to set out the dining setting.

Abbie was watching him, and stopped to stare. It was Robbo, all spruced up and clean. He was a completely different person to what he had seemed at the park. Quite good looking in fact. He even winked at her when her mother wasn't looking.

Victoria was just shooing him off when Abbie thought to ask, "Mum, can I get some Pepsi instead of cider? Just his once?"

Victoria nodded tensely, and Abbie grinned back at Robbo as he promised to bring it quickly. When he had gone, Victoria said, "Darling, he's just a waiter. He is not someone you need to throw yourself at."

"Mum, I wasn't! It was just a bit of harmless pretend."

"Some men think that's enough of an invitation – or have you forgotten what nearly happened not so long ago?"

"No. Is Dad going to make you cloister me like a nun?"

"Of course not! He'll see that you get to meet suitable young men, but all in good time. You are still very young."

"Didn't you ever do some harmless flirting with boys at my age?" Abbie knew she had done more than that.

"Abbie, dear, I probably did, and I learnt some hard lessons then too. I don't want you to have to do the same."

The food took on a new fascination while her mother talked about nice looking boys and all they wanted from a girl. Finally, Abbie dared to ask, "What was so different about Daddy? He's good looking."

Robbo returned with her drink before her mother answered. Abbie hopped up to go to the door. "I'll get it. You are my chaperone anyway.”

The sarcasm went over Victoria’s head. She just watched as she politely thanked the waiter, but didn’t see the envelope that passed with the can. She closed and locked the door, as she slipped the envelope out of sight.

“Daddy!” Abbie pretended to be ecstatic when her mother opened the door for him. She ran and gave him a big hug, and pretended not to feel how tense he was as he automatically patted her back and gave her a perfunctory kiss on the top of her head.

“You look glamorous,” he remarked after Victoria asked him what he thought of her new look. His smile, directed at her, lasted just that long. “Now, why don’t you go and watch something on Netflix? I need to talk to your Mum.”

The sense of something wrong came rushing over her. However, she pretended that she was oblivious, and trotted across to the couch to get the TV remote control. As if this was a delightful treat! She turned the volume up, more than usual, so she wasn’t surprised when her father said, “Turn that down a bit, will you, Abbie?”

“Sure, Dad. I’ll use the headphones.”

The show she had chosen lost its appeal, so while plugging in the earphones, she turned the volume way down. When her father checked, he would think she couldn’t hear anything. At first she didn’t, but when her mother’s voice got louder, so did her father’s. If she kept looking at the TV, he wouldn’t think she could hear. His voice carried, and with one ear slightly uncovered, she was an avid listener.

It seemed that he needed to explain something to her mother. How she needed to respond to certain questions. Her mother should have been an actress, she learned quickly. Usually she didn’t ask her own questions about what or why he wanted something, but this time her father’s behaviour must seem stranger than normal, even to her.

"Just remember, Abbie is my daughter. Her mother died when she was little. The department contacted me and we were happy to take her in."

"Then why will they be coming now?" Victoria's voice was shrill. "Are they going to take my little girl away?"

"They can't," Carson assured her. "I'm her father."

"Then why didn't you marry her mother?"

"Victoria, we had already decided to separate, before she realised she was pregnant. She wanted the baby. In fact, I think she seduced me. I did what I could for her, paid the doctor's bills and the hospital bills and helped get all the stuff for the baby. Once she'd had it, she moved away. I lost track of her."

"But why do they want to question you now?"

"Well, it seems the girl came into some money. She wasn't anything like you. She was totally unsophisticated. Her parents or someone invested it. Now they are getting on, they finally decided to find her bastard child. Or that is all I can presume. Obviously they weren't interested in the child back then, or why did the department hunt me up?"

"Oh," Victoria subsided. Abbie thought her mother must be trying to take all that in.

"So, tomorrow, I have an appointment with the Hartley Trustees. They'll want to meet Abbie. She will need to be well dressed and polite. Make that clear to her."

"Yes, Jeremy. She looks great with the new hairstyle, doesn't she?"

"She does," Carson agreed. "Now, remember all I said. This is an investment that I have had growing for over ten years. Once the Trustees are sure of Abbie, they will be giving her an allowance until she is eighteen, and then she will inherit the Hartley fortune. That's over two billion dollars right now. They will need someone to make sure she doesn't meet shysters out to fleece her. Who else but the father who brought her up and given her a stable home life? We will be set for life. I'll never have to work again."

Abbie's mind as reeling at the size of the inheritance she was supposedly meant to get. His last statement jolted her. "*What?*" her mind exclaimed. She stopped listening to her parents talking. She went over the things he had said, and what she had recently learnt about Maude Hartley. Some things didn't add up, but them Gail might have had her facts wrong, or she had twisted the truth to be nasty. The newspapers might have their facts wrong.

She had her iPad handy and logged into the hotel Wi-Fi. It came up first with her private gmail account, Annie saying hi and sending English notes. Abbie scowled. Little innocent Annie, she thought. Going on to think, "I bet old mad Maude was just like her at fifteen. Ripe to be conned."

She switched to the browser, and began a search for information on the Hartley's. She had a second page opened on a search for fashion schools, in case her father came near. He hadn't reacted negatively to that as a future career. He knew she was good at maths, like he was, but didn't think maths led to a career for a 'lady'. He always encouraged her to be more like her mother.

A decoration! Useless at everything, her mind retorted. Having to rely on a man to give her everything. Robbo's story had given her a new outlook into possibilities —women could be milked dry, and then discarded.

Chapter 3

Abbie heard her father get up and quickly switched to a fashion website.

"I'll see you both tomorrow," Carson told Victoria before coming over. She used the remote to pause her show, and took off the earphones.

"Can we go home tomorrow, Daddy?" she asked.

"We'll see. I just need you to be well dressed tomorrow afternoon. You and I have an important meeting."

"I don't know what to wear. I didn't bring anything really good with me."

"I'll let your mother take you shopping."

"What's the meeting about, Daddy? Something to do with your work?"

"I will explain tomorrow, but if all goes well, it may mean you can choose which ever fashion college you want to go to."

"Really?" Abbie bounced up and down, deciding to act both childish and excited. Her father merely nodded, seeming satisfied. He gave her another perfunctory kiss before heading for the door. Abbie jumped up and followed him.

"Get a good night's sleep, okay?" he said before closing the door on her.

Abbie turned off the show that she had been pretending to watch and said she was going to bed. It was still early, only eight, but she wanted to think. She had skimmed through a lot of articles about the Hartley family and the sole remaining member, Maude.

That was one thing her father had lied about. Maude Hartley, her supposed mother, was still alive. Admittedly, twelve years ago, she'd been committed to some mental institution, and no one expected her to be released, ever. Did her father equate that with dead? Or did he not want to be known to have had sex with a poor simple minded woman? But the committal might have been why she had been brought to him. But surely he had read about her in the newspapers recently? If he had, he would know she wasn't dead or incarcerated. She had never dared trying to read his paper before he did, and he never seemed to leave them lying around. At school though, they were encouraged to keep up with current affairs. The library got copies of each day's newspapers.

The story he had told her mother was a complete fabrication. Maude Hartley had two girls, not just one. Her father hadn't even mentioned the other. Okay, the other one was supposed to be dead now, but he should have mentioned that. And the newspapers said her parents had died before her girls were born, so she had been an heiress already. She probably didn't look rich, but her father had said something about an investment of a decade. So he had to have known what she was and had been one of the sort of men he was claiming to be keeping away from her.

She continued to analyse the conversation and it was his final statement, "We'll be set for life, won't have to work' that seemed to settle the point.

She felt sick. If she was an heiress, then he was after her inheritance. What should she do?

Then she thought of the envelope in her pocket, and felt for it.

"Hi Sis, didn't expect to see you. But I get off work soon. Let us know if we can help, okay? Here's twenty dollars if you need it for bus fare. If you need somewhere to go, our offer is still open. Take a tram..." Abbie memorised the directions, and checked the phone number with the one she had. Robbo had finished with, "If you decide to come, call us and we'll meet you."

Her decision crystallised. She wanted no part in her father's scam. Not when it meant that once he had her money, he would probably up and disappear. She would go away, and when the police found her this time she would tell them why she had needed to get away.

Her mind made up, Abbie grabbed her back pack and sorted out what she needed to take. A change of clothes, her iPad and phones, their chargers, her purse with her remaining loose cash, a bottle of water from beside her bed, and that was about all that would fit.

She would have to pretend she had gone to bed, for her mother would probably check. It wouldn't seem odd that she was asleep already. It had been a very long day. Then once her mother had been in, and had gone to bed and was asleep. That was when she would leave. In the meantime, she could check she knew where the tram and bus stops were to get to Footscray.

Hearing the toilet flushing in the ensuite, warned Abbie to feign sleep. She heard her door opening quietly, and a minute later, closing again. She'd wait half an hour, then get dressed in her new jeans and the other stuff she'd bought in NSW. It was probably going to get cool, so her new hoodie would be useful.

Leaving was easy, she unlocked the door and set it to auto relock when she closed it. Now, she couldn't go back in! The hotel passages were deserted, and the lobby only had the dim security lights. It seemed that anyone who was going to arrive, had done so already. Still, she was careful to look around before crossing to the main door. That was locked, but the revolving door still went around. That was all she needed. Once out, she scurried for the nearest patch of shadow and looked around.

The city was quiet, but there were still cars and trucks

moving on the street. A few pedestrians too. People coming from restaurants or the cinema. She moved along with one such group, a little bit behind, until she found the tram stop she wanted. There she looked for the timetable to tell her when the next tram was due. The one she wanted was going to be a while. She hadn't thought of that. Looking around, she decided to wait in the shelter of a doorway. Some of the loitering people were a bit off putting. She didn't want to be noticed.

She watched a figure walking along the far side of the road. If she had to guess, she would say it was a woman. Some of the uncouth looking men started to follow her, one came up beside her. Abbie couldn't hear what the woman said, but the man quickly dropped back, and after watching her move on, turned and ran off the other way.

Then the figure came to the kerb, looked both ways and scampered across the road, dodging cars. Abbie, feeling superior, told herself that she knew better than to do such a stupid thing. She continued to watch the woman, as she neared. She couldn't see her face, for she seemed to be watching the ground, but when she drew next to the tram stop, she went across the near side of the road to the central space for people to get on and off the tram.

Then, she seemed to lean against the barrier and look around. Abbie gasped in surprise. She knew the woman.

"Wanda?" she said softly to herself, almost not believing it. What incredible luck! What was she doing here, at this hour?

Chapter 4

"Hi!"

Wanda turned, wondering if the voice meant her. Vague memories were moving sluggishly into focus. A name bubbled up.

"Oh, hi. Abbie, right?"

"Yes. What happened to you?"

Something like a mirror reflection entered her mind. Wanda felt the side of her head where a dull ache lingered. The vision had shown dried blood.

"Nothing of importance. I'm functional. What are you doing out here at this hour?"

"Going to visit my brother and sister. I'm waiting for the tram. What about you?"

That was a question Wanda couldn't answer yet. "Mooching around. How come you are going now? Next tram's not for an half an hour and it's not safe for a young thing like you."

"I can look after myself," Abbie insisted. "Should you go to a doctor?"

"Told you, I'm functional. Where are you going on the tram?"

"Footscray."

"Want company? I ain't got anywhere special to go."

"Thought you had a boyfriend. Did he kick you out?"

"Yeah," Wanda decided to agree, although the answer felt wrong. "Wouldn't mind company for a while. Do you reckon your brother would let me crash there for the night?"

"I can ask," Abbie promised, realising she was relieved to have company too. Especially as a couple of unsavoury looking men were calling at them. She wondered what Wanda had said to the others to make them want to get right away.

They waited in silence after that. Abbie kept checking her watch for something to do.

"I tried calling you earlier," Abbie commented, not peevishly, because she could see the woman was hurt.

Wanda felt for her phone. "Must have lost my phone somewhere."

"I got myself a new phone," Abbie said. "Dad changed my plan on the other one, and my number. So I got an Optus prepaid with tons of data and included calls. Daddy can't keep looking into who I call and what I look up on the internet."

"What's your new number then, kid?"

Abbie considered for a moment, then rattled it off. "Do you need to write it down?"

"No, I'll remember."

A tram rattled around the corner.

"This is it," Abbie confirmed. "Have you got a myki card?"

Wanda checked her pocket and pulled out a flat wallet. The card slots had various cards in them. What each was flashed into her mind.

"Yeah." The card was black, and her mind spat out how she was meant to touch on and off. Things were beginning to come back to her.

The tram only had a few other travellers. Abbie went to the front, near the driver's door, and well away from the other people. Wanda put her myki card away and checked the other cards. Her face stared up at her from an International Driver's Licence. David had made her get it, even though she didn't intend to drive here.

David...he was important. She read her name, "Wanda Martin."

Slipping that card away, she looked at the next. It was her US State Department ID. More memories surfaced. She remembered someone yanking an ID off her neck. She concentrated on that face, and the room behind it. She felt in her pocket as a memory of snatching it back surfaced. A card attached to a lanyard met her fingers, but this time the memory came unprompted.

"We get off next stop," Abbie nudged her.

Wanda looked around. "Where's here?"

"Robbo lives in a street a couple of blocks from here."

The name brought more memories, initially of Abbie, telling her about her brother, and also of the arrogant bloke who thought he could intimidate her.

"You sure you want to be there?" Wanda asked. "What'll your old man do?"

"I don't care. I don't want to be part of his filthy scam."

Whatever had been affecting her, vanished - abruptly. Memories flicked through her mind....Carson!

"What's this? What's he making you do?"

"Pretend to be someone," Abbie said defensively. "The kid of some mad person. My friends will all sneer at me."

"And your old man will have the cops all looking for you. You'll probably end up having your face plastered all over the newspapers."

"I won't. Come on."

Abbie checked the instruction for where to go next, while under a streetlight. Wanda let her lead the way.

"You got your other phone on you too?" Wanda asked abruptly.

"Yeah, but it's turned off."

"Let me have it."

"Why?"

"Because if your old man can track your phone, and its usage, it may not matter if it's turned on or not. I'll take the sim card out."

Alarmed, Abbie complied. "Will that stop it?"

"I think so," Wanda told her, not saying that it might be too late already. "What time did you leave home?"

"Dad made mum and me stay in a hotel in town. I waited until mum was asleep. So about eleven or half past."

Wanda checked her watch. It was broken and had stopped

displaying the time. What had happened to her?

One house had a light on outside and its number agreed with that on Abbie's written directions. Now she stopped, as if uncertain what to do.

"We can't stay here all night," Wanda prodded. "Come on."

Wanda strode to the door, and as she had expected, Abbie scurried after her. She knocked quietly, but in the night stillness, she heard sounds of movement within. The curtain covering the window near the door, twitched. Then the door opened.

"You!" Robbo exclaimed, seeing Wanda. "I didn't invite you. Just the little Sis."

"Too bad. You ain't no kinda brother encouraging a girl her age to come visiting you at night."

"Didn't tell her to come at night," Robbo countered.

"Well, she did, and we're here, so let us in," Wanda insisted.

The door opened further, and he moved aside to let them in. Then he shut and locked the door and doused the outside light.

"Thanks for seeing she got here safe," Thea came and gave Abbie hug. "What's the bastard done now?" She began to shepherd Abbie into another room. "You can sleep in my room."

"You can go now," Robbo told Wanda. "We don't need you around."

"No? What's going to happen when her old man finds out she ain't around?"

"What do you know?"

"Bits. Look, I need a place to flop tonight. And if her old man knows where you are and sends cops, I can say she came here on her own."

Robbo stared. "Alright. Pick a bit of floor, but the little sis won't be harmed. She's a bargaining piece."

"Right," Wanda's tone suggested disbelief. "Reckon that's all she is to her old man too. He's up to some super-scam, sounds like."

"Nothing new," Robbo agreed. "But if you're right, he'll be more willing to pay up, I reckon."

"Probably send the police."

"And you can say your piece. We couldn't kick her out this late, could we?"

Wanda grinned at him. "Wouldn't be real nice if you did."

Robbo grinned back. "Carson, as he calls himself now, deserves to be put in jail."

"Ever thought to go to the police about him?"

"Nah. We hired a lawyer. He said too much time's gone past. So we're doing some sort of civil thing. But he wouldn't listen and denied knowing us. He slapped some order on us, so we can't go near him. Lawyer did say we should try negotiating with him."

"So he scammed you, did he?" Wanda switched directions for the conversation.

"Yeah. Took all our Mum's inheritance, sold her house, took our college funds, all mum's shares and things. Left us with nothing."

"You know," Wanda pointed a finger at Robbo. "That guy's beginning to reek so much that I can smell him from here."

The phone ringing by his bead startled Carson to instant wakefulness.

"Hello?" he answered cautiously.

"Jeremy! It's me. I can't find Abbie! She's not in the suite. Some of her stuff is missing too."

"How can she be missing?" he demanded, fear coursing through him.

"She was in bed! I checked on her before I turned in. I got up just now, and her door was ajar, so I looked in."

"Wait a moment, Victoria. Now, you have looked everywhere?"

"Yes, of course I did."

"Has she been calling any of her friends?"

"No."

"Let me check," Carson insisted. He reached for his smart phone and opened the family safe app, and put in Abbie's new number. No, she'd hardly used the phone since she'd left, and hadn't tried to go online. He opened another window in the app and checked her location.

The receiver at his ear spluttered as Victoria said, "Oh, Jeremy, she was flirting with a waiter. I told her it was unbecoming and a waiter was beneath her."

Carson only partly listened as he stared at the screen. How had that stupid little twit got to Footscray?

"What was that?" he demanded, and Victoria repeated what she had said. "What was he like?"

"Oh, dark haired, good looking, tallish," Victoria said. It wasn't a really good description, but the son he'd ditched long ago, had dark hair. But if the bastard who was trying to blackmail him now, had cleaned himself up...he'd planned this!

"Victoria, calm down! I will get in touch with hotel security. They can check the hotel. She has probably snuck out to see him. You stay there in case she calls, returns, or I hear something. Security may need to ask for more details. Will you do that?"

"Yes, Jeremy, of course. Oh, I do hope she's alright."

"She won't be if I get hold of her," Carson growled. "She will be lucky if I only send her to a convent boarding school."

"Oh, Jeremy, no!"

"Victoria, the girl needs to learn sense and responsibility. We've been too lenient with her. Now, let me hang up and make that call."

He had hardly time to find the number when the house phone rang. He didn't go to answer it, since who would be calling at this hour? He let the answering machine take it.

"Are you missing something, Father?" He recognised the smart ass voice of the caller, and wanted to snarl. The call ended before he could reach the handset.

Carson didn't immediately make any calls, He needed to think, to be calm.

If those two claiming to be his children, had Abbie, they would probably not hurt her. They would want her to be cooperative, so they could use her to get their way.

Well, he wasn't going to give them a cent. They only thought they were his kids. They didn't know their mother had been playing around back then. He'd turned a blind eye. It kept her happy when he was away on business. Besides, she and the kids had been good window dressing. He owed them nothing.

How could he turn this to his advantage? They could be blamed for abducting her, or luring her away, and if he snatched her back, they would not be able to say anything. They were meant to have been keeping away from her and Victoria too. They would still be guilty of putting her in danger.

Yes! He'd get Mickey to go and get her back. 50K would be worth it to solve a few problems at one stroke. He would need to set up some ransom messages. It would give him reason to get out the money in used bills like Mickey wanted. He couldn't go near those two himself, but Mickey wanted to get away, seemed desperate enough, he would come through.

Now, where to stash the girl? Yes, that second storage unit he had arranged in their name, where he'd stashed some of the valuable stuff from his house. Then they'd be blamed for robbery too. He would be in the clear, the frantic parent. Good PR for himself with the trustees.

If Mickey was caught, he'd not talk if he wanted his money. He wouldn't be believed anyway, after all, he'd married Maude and it might be thought he had ideas of getting her money.

The police would believe the abduction – perhaps he would have a note delivered in the morning? He'd insist on getting the money ready to exchange...

Mickey just needed to get the girl to the unit. And when she was found, in that unit, the renters traced...those extortionists would not be believed.

And the little chit wouldn't be able to get out. There was some bottled water there, and tinned food. A day or two wouldn't hurt her, and it would be a lesson for her. Obey him because he knew best.

Having thought it all out, Carson dialled Long Lonny's place where Mickey was now staying.

"There's a problem, Abbie has disappeared. You have to help me get her back. If I can't produce her, looking happy and well, there will be no money."

"I don't care, Carson," Delaney hissed. "You promised me 50K and we'd be quits. That's for all the stuff I did for you twelve years ago."

"I know! But I was going to have to borrow on other assets to get it," Carson lied easily.

"But you live in that fancy house," Mickey sneered.

"Of course I do. Who would take my investment advice if I lived in a hovel. I only rent it. Now, will you do as I say? I know where she is likely to be, with those two who are trying to extort money from me. You wouldn't want them to succeed, would you?"

Delaney hissed a gutter curse. "Alright but the police are already looking for me. And I will need a couple of thousand to pay the help."

"Mickey, tell the help not to talk," Carson warned. "I know who the police will believe, and I have friends high up in the police force. Don't be caught or it will be goodbye 50k."

"Where do you reckon she'll be?" Mickey capitulated.

"In Footscray, 27A Charles Street." That was the address where he had discovered his former children were living.

"What if she's not there?"

"She will be. The two living there have as good as admitted it. I have a recording of a call they made me."

"Okay, where do you want me to take her?"

"I have a storage unit. Not in my name. Behind the Herald street shops. You should know it. No 17. There is a lock on it, but I didn't lock it properly.

"Are you trying to get me caught? The cops are all over that area like fleas on a dog."

"If you want your money Mickey, you'll do it. And you won't need to stay with her there." Carson told him. "If I am sure Abbie won't be found for a day or two, and I get a ransom note in my letterbox, then I have an unimpeachable reason to get 50K out in notes. Get it?"

Carson smiled grimly, when he heard Mickey chuckle on the other end of the phone. "You're setting up those two who want to screw you, aren't you."

Carson just laughed.

Only after he had organised everything with Mickey, did Carson call to talk to the hotel's security. He said he would be coming into town, but could they look around for his daughter who might be flirting with one of the waiters, and he gave the description Victoria had given him. He asked for a delay before notifying the police, as his daughter was going through a rebellious phase, and he didn't want to make a huge fuss if she was still within the hotel. He knew the hotel did not want the adverse publicity.

After a day of doing nothing but drinking, Mickey was getting edgy. He had hoped to have heard from Carson already. He wanted to be away. He went to bed cursing Carson, and determined to force him to pay up.

It was the middle of the night when Lonny roughly shook him awake.

"Tell your mate I'm not your answering service," Lonny complained. He liked his sleep.

Mickey rolled over and reached for the phone. He checked the number, it was from a mobile.

"Yeah! Wassit?"

Recognising Carson's voice, he sat up. "This better be good. You got my money?"

"There's a problem, Abbie has disappeared. You have to help me get her back. If I can't produce her, looking happy and well, there will be no money."

"I don't care Carson," Delaney hissed. "You promised me 50K and we'd be quits. That's for all the stuff I did for you twelve years ago."

"I know! But I was going to have to borrow on other assets to get it."

"But you live in that fancy house," Mickey sneered. It was bullshit. Carson had multiple bank accounts.

"Of course I do. Who would take my investment advice if I lived in a hovel? I only rent it. Now, will you do as I say? I know where she is likely to be, with those two who are trying to extort money from me. You wouldn't want them to succeed, would you?"

Delaney hissed a gutter curse. The hell he wouldn't. Not until Carson had paid him. Then they could clean him out. "Alright but the police are already looking for me. And I will need a couple of thousand to pay the help."

Mickey snarled back at Carson, and his warnings about talking. Of course he wouldn't and those he would call to help wouldn't either. "Where do you reckon she'll be?" he capitulated. He listened and then said, "You're setting up those two who want to screw you, aren't you."

Carson just laughed. "And supposedly they have hired a storage unit – one around here near the shops. No 17. The key is under a piece of cracked concrete, just around the side in the lane."

Mickey had sobered up by the time he was dressed and went into roust Kemple.

"Want to earn a hundred quid?"

"What? Oh, yeah. I'm in it." Kemple woke quickly. "What's the job?"

"My mate has a little problem," Mickey began, and he gave Kemple the gist. "Can you ring Ossi and Crane? We need a fast set of wheels, with a big boot and stuff to disguise our faces. Make it two cars."

Kemple took out his phone and began the ring around.

"Ossi's crook. Got the runs," he reported after the first call.

"Call Whacko then, and Manfred too," Mickey directed.

"They'll be here in fifteen minutes," Kemple reported finally.

Mickey grinned, seeing the two fast looking, newly stolen cars. A BMW and a Ford. The Ford would do for Footscray, the other for the return when they switched cars. He quickly briefed the three newcomers, gave them directions, and the five of them split between the two cars.

Once underway, with Manfred driving the BMW, Mickey got his knives out and ensured they were handy. He looked at the gear Whacko had collected – usually had on hand. Chloroform and cloth, ropes to tie up the girl, tape for her mouth, a blanket to cover her from sight. Whacko would probably try for a grope, but all the more to scare the girl into silence.

The cars both pulled into the Footscray railway station carpark. Kemple had headed for a dark area, seemingly by instinct. They left the BMW unlocked, and Mickey had everyone take a stocking, and get it ready to pull over their faces. He tucked the chloroform and cloth in his pocket, and patted the knives in their hidden sheaths. All climbed into the Ford and Kemple followed the directions of the inbuilt GPS. At Mickey's direction, he drove past the house first, and did a turn, so they were on the right side of the street and pointed for a quick getaway.

Mickey was already anticipating the raid. The girl wouldn't recognise him, even if he wasn't disguised. Her father for a few months, years ago? He wondered how like her stupid mother she was. Maybe he could make her mad too? He pulled his mind back to the job.

"Okay, Crane, you and Manfred go in the back. Whacko, you and I will take the front. Kemple, you have the car ready to go. You know the way back to the station?"

"Course I do. I grew up here."

Mickey counted slowly to twenty. Crane had an excellent time sense. "Now," he directed Whacko softly.

Whacko had a gun out as his huge booted foot kicked the door in. The dim light from the street light was enough to be aware of a figure springing up from the couch in the front room. The figure stopped, when Mickey growled, "Where's the girl."

He thought it was a man, probably the psycho Carson was out to frame.

A scream came from a room further in. Mickey dived that way, leaving Whacko to deal with the first obstacle. The scream stopped, and someone erupted from a room beside him, bellowing, "What's going on?"

Wanting no one to stop him, Mickey acted immediately, knifing the figure before pushing him backwards. He strode forward to where Crane had one girl gagged with one arm and immobilised against him. Another girl was sprawled against a wall, trying to stand again. Mickey took out the cloth and poured chloroform onto it. Carson's kid tried to struggle, but hadn't a hope to get the cloth from her face.

He heard another bellow, as the man who didn't know he should be dead, rushed into the room. Mickey turned and back handed him. To Manfred he said, "Finish him!" as he took the groggy girl and tossed her over his shoulder. Something began pounding on his back, and again he swung around, this time to punch his new tormentor.

He turned to head out to the car, only to see the way blocked by the figure from the front room. The light was on now, and he recognised the woman who had humiliated him. He dropped the girl, and said, "Get her to the car," he ordered his mates. He had a passing thought of "Where was Whacko?" as the horrid voice of the woman asked, "Want another lesson, cockroach?"

His knife was out and he was lunging forward, his blood boiling with the desire to finish her. Yet she seemed unworried, and he quickly found out why. Her foot hit his wrist, and the knife went flying from his hand.

Manfred ran to get a clear line of fire at this unexpected assailant, but his target moved. He saw her arm jerk, so he had at least grazed her. Mickey used that moment to reach forward and grab that arm, expecting her to black out from pain, but he was wrong. It seemed to unleash a spring on the other arm, and her fist hit him on the bridge of his nose, and something poked his eye.

"Stop her following," Mickey roared to Manfred, as he stumbled to the door, and then headed for the car that had its door open ready.

He didn't wait to see what Manfred did, he knew the bitch wasn't hurt badly, and would be after him. "Get going!" he ordered Kemple, and the car revved forward with immediate ferocity.

Episode 16

Where is Abbie?

Chapter 1

Lights had come on in the neighbouring houses, and a few tentative figures were peering out doors and windows. The screaming and the gunshot probably meant cops were on the way. He waited until they were two blocks away before telling Kemple, "Slow down."

He looked the back seat to check Crane had the girl down out of sight.

"What! I hear sirens," Kemple said, his voice shaking.

"Slow down! Take the next left and pull into the curb. Turn your lights off and take your foot off the brake!"

Mickey waited until a police car, with lights and siren, raced past the street. "Okay, get going. Take it easy. The station isn't far. Once we switch cars, we're safe."

Crane and Mickey kept their faces covered until they reached the station. The girl had stopped struggling, now the chloroform had worked. Kemple had indeed picked a good place to have the BMW parked. They were out of the way of the station's security lights and cameras. They transferred the girl to the boot of the BMW, covered by the blanket, and each put their stocking mask into a pocket and kept their gloves on.

Once again, they waited until an ambulance went roaring down the main road. Then with Crane driving instead of the shaking Kemple, they drove sedately back towards the city and the inner eastern suburbs.

They reached Bellfield and pulled into a street near the shops. "Go and get the key for unit 17. It's under a loose piece of paving," Mickey told Kemple. "Unlock it and be ready to lift the roller door."

He and Crane had begun to drive towards the unit when they saw Kemple trotting back. "Cops. A marked car watching the shops, and a plain one near the park. There may be more," he puffed when the van stopped. "What will we do?"

"Let me think!" Delaney silenced him.

Carson just wanted the girl out of the way for a day or two. The storage unit idea was perfect. It put suspicion on the punk kids. With cops around, though, it was too risky. Okay, there would be a way.

A loud ping, startled him. "Did you check that girl for a phone?" he demanded, twisting to stare at Crane, who immediately bent down to frisk the girl. He held up a phone.

"Take it out and dump it," Mickey said at once, handing it to Kemple. "Take one of her shoes as well. Leave the shoe near unit 17, and have the phone off before you dump it. Meet us back at Lonny's."

"Where are we going to put her?" a fidgety Kemple insisted.

"Your place!"

"But the kid will see," Kemple whined.

"If he sees us and comes out, I'll be waiting."

"What if he calls the cops instead? He seems to be chummy with them now."

"Ok, we'll go to that empty Chinese joint for now. If the girl wakes up, we can give her more stuff to knock her out. We'll tie her up and tape her mouth. We'll go to your place, after your kid's gone to school. Okay?"

Kemple nodded and moved the car to the service alley at the shops. He parked between two delivery cars and a grocery truck. A moment's work on the back lock of the empty shop, had it open and Kemple gestured Mickey in with his burden.

"Drive the car to the nearest station and get back to Lonny's. Crane, we'll need a new set of wheels – a van or the like, for later. We'd best be gone from here by eight."

Mickey knew exactly how far Kemple could be trusted, and that point was well past. He was a right coward unless suitably motivated.

He locked the door and watched through one of the dirty rear windows as Kemple went off. Then he moved the girl out of the kitchen and into the area once used for dining. She was still out cold, so he did a look around to see what he could find.

Delaney spent the rest of the night pacing the vacant former Chinese restaurant, and keeping an eye out for police activity. Once he heard the back door being shaken, and footsteps going off. He wanted a smoke, but he had none with him and he didn't know if the place had smoke alarms either. He occupied his mind wondering if Carson had known of the police activity and was wanting him caught. Then he decided, no, Carson was trying to get those kids of his in trouble.

When his prisoner began to stir, struggling so much that she nearly had the rug off, he went and kicked her in the thigh.

"Shut up and stop wriggling," he told her in a low growl. "You make a noise, I will break your back and then use you for fun."

As he expected, the girl became a silent quivering heap. His phone vibrated in his pocket. He strode from the open area to where he could talk in private. He had already sent Carson a text saying, "Done". However when he saw he number and recognised the number of Carson's untraceable mobile – he decided not to answer. An idea had occurred to him. Carson could do a much better 'worried about his kid' act if he really didn't know where she was. He was wanting those two punks blamed. They didn't know anything, and would of course deny everything and not be believed. But that other bitch...she was a problem. Even disguised, she had somehow recognised him. He should have finished her. Maybe Manfred had, but she had taken Whacko down and out. The cops probably had Manfred too. One thing was urgently imperative. That woman might talk; she'd have to be fixed.

And Carson, he'd be all the more desperate to pay up, if he didn't know where the kid was. The question was, how was he was going to play it if he decided to bring the cops into it. He had seemed sure that he'd be able to get the used bills for a ransom. Well, one thing was sure, Carson had better not expect him to make an exchange if cops were around. He would have to talk to Carson, find a way to get the money on the side. Maybe, have everyone concentrating on the drop site, while he went into Carson's house and took his money from there. What was he planning to do anyway?

He activated his now silent phone and poked the redial button for the last caller.

"Yes?" was all Carson said as an answer.

"You alone?" Mickey asked, his voice hoarse due to the swelling around his nose.

"Give me a moment." Mickey heard him excusing himself. Then, "I haven't long. You have her?"

"Yes but not where you said. Cops were around. Call me back when no one is around." Mickey ended the call.

Thinking some more, he decided that he wouldn't tell Carson where she was. Not until he had his money. Maybe not even then.

At the first sound of the men bursting into the rented house, Wanda sprang up from the couch where she had fallen asleep. There was a gun pointed at her, only mere inches from her face.

"Where's the girl?" a stocking garbled voice demanded.

Wanda didn't need to answer. A scream from another room was abruptly cut off, to be replaced by a scuffle. More men must have come in the back door. One of the men watching her went towards the noises. A roar from Robbo became another scuffle.

Wanda saw the gunman in front of her glance that way, and sprang. Adrenalin blasting along her veins, cleared the last of the drug induced fuzziness from her. The man fell, making little sound, and Wanda frisked him for other weapons. She took a knife, and the man's gun.

A man was dragging a struggling Abbie into view, and another man had Thea by her hair. One of them roared, "Finish him!" to the figure struggling with Robbo.

Knowledge of who that man was, came to Wanda like a revelation – Mickey Delaney!

None of those three had seen her, and she shoved the one holding Thea into Mickey. He had to release Thea, to get free of Mickey, and Thea began to pound on Mickey's back. A bad idea, for he simply swung around and punched the side of her neck. Thea went limp.

When Mickey Delaney turned around again, and saw her, and his eyes went wide with unholy glee.

He shoved Abbie at one of the other men. "Get her to the car!" Then he drew a wickedly sharp looking knife.

"Want another lesson, cockroach?" Wanda taunted, expecting a physical attack as a rush from Delaney. She did not hear the slight sound of a gun being drawn, only the shot and the seemingly simultaneous searing pain.

Mickey, thinking to disable her easily, and anticipating slipping his knife into her, grabbed the injured arm, only to discover his mistake. She wasn't weakened, and her left fist hit him hard, between the eyes.

It was enough. "Stop that bitch following," Mickey ordered, as he made for the front door. As soon as Mickey turned his back, his accomplice discovered that she still wasn't stopped. He reached to grab, and couldn't have said how he ended on the floor. He had little time to think, before being unconscious.

Wanda ran outside, just as the car in the street revved off, wheels spinning for a moment. She only had a fleeting glimpse of the car's numberplate. Then Thea began screaming and Wanda raced back inside.

"Shut up!" she roared at Thea. "What's wrong?"

"Robbo! He's dead."

"Where?"

Thea pointed. Wanda found him bleeding badly from a stab wound. She was instantly in paramedic mode, feeling for a pulse and finding one.

"Get some towels or pillow slips," Wanda ordered. "Hurry! He's still alive."

Thea ran off, opening a cupboard and grabbing what came to hand. She practically threw the bundle at Wanda.

"Can you call for an ambulance?"

Thea nodded and fumbled for her phone, realised it was by her bed and ran to the nearer landline.

"But the police will come," Thea wailed.

"Damn right!" Wanda said without sympathy. "Or have you not realised they took Abbie?"

When Thea still dithered, Wanda said, "Come here! Keep pressure on this. Give me the phone."

She almost dialled 911, but recalled that Australia used 000.

When the operator answered, she requested the ambulance and gave a succinct explanation of the situation. Then she asked for the police. When she was connected, she immediately identified herself, using her Atlas task force credentials. When she asked to be connected to Kelso's number, she was connected at once. His phone began to ring and every second she waited seemed like a minute. She needed to get back to Robbo.

"Task force, David speaking."

"Get to 27A Charles Street, Footscray. Robbo's been knifed, bad. Abbie Carson taken by Mickey Delaney," she added the info on the car they left in, then added, "Ambo coming, but need regular police too."

She didn't give David time for questions, just hung up and ran back to Robbo. He had begun to moan.

"Stay still, Robbo," she told him firmly. "You are losing blood, but help is coming."

"Will he be alright?" Thea wailed.

"I hope so," Wanda told her, taking over keeping the pressure on, knowing that the knife had nicked the intestine – from the smell. She distracted the girl. "You're bleeding too? What happened?"

Thea seemed dazed, and was probably going into shock. She wasn't as tough as she had tried to make out. "I don't know. One had a knife. What about you? There's a lot of blood on your sleeve."

"A graze," Wanda knew. A deep one, but the bullet hadn't gone in. She could hear sirens, getting closer. "Go open the door," Wanda ordered.

The confusion of paramedics and police was peripheral as Wanda succinctly described the wound. The local paramedics took over smoothly. One asked, as he worked, "You've had training."

"Yes. I am a qualified paramedic in California."

"This guy is lucky you were here."

"I hope his luck holds."

Wanda stood up and realised that someone had thrown the throw rug from the couch around Thea. She went to where she stood shaking so hard she couldn't speak, and took her in a hug.

The senior detective who had responded, spoke behind her. "You'd be Mrs Davis then?"

Wanda nodded, and urged Thea to the couch, and into sitting down.

"I have instructions for you to stay here until some of my colleagues arrive, but I see that you are hurt too."

"A graze," Wanda claimed again. "I don't need the hospital. You need to put a call out for a light coloured Ford. Rego starts with ABE. Mickey Delaney and a few of his mates burst in here. They took a girl called Abbie Carson. Oh, I see your partner has found the two that couldn't leave."

"Yes, we had a report that the Carson girl was here."

"Who from? Carson?"

The detective nodded. Wanda thought to ask, "Sorry, I didn't catch your name?"

"Thatcher," the man said.

Wanda turned to Thea and asked, "Did Robbo call him to gloat?"

"He...he...might have."

"Either that or he has an app to track her phone. He knows Robbo and Thea, and probably knows they are staying here."

"Abbie's phone is in the other room," Thea said. The shuddering was beginning to ease.

"We'll need a statement about what happened here," Thatcher announced.

"We didn't bring her," Thea protested at once. "We just said she was welcome if she wanted to get away from her father.

Our father too, that is.”

“Why’d you bring her, Mrs Davis?”

“She was already more than half way here anyway, and I wanted to talk to Robbo and her.”

“Why?” Thea asked. “I didn’t even know you until you arrived.”

“Your brother and I have met before.”

Thatcher turned his attention to the paramedics, who had Robbo on the trolley, and a drip in his arm, and were wheeling him out. “Where will you be taking him?”

“Western General,” was the terse answer.

Thatcher gestured to one of the uniformed police who had arrived. “Go with him.”

“Thea should go too,” Wanda said. “She has a slash on her arm.”

The police officer nodded, and directed Thea to leave with him.

Once Thea was out of the house, Wanda ignored the detective's next question, and went into the bedroom to examine where Thea and Abbie had been sleeping. She found Abbie's phone, the one she'd removed the card from, in the small shoulder bag.

"What are you doing?" Thatcher asked sharply.

"Checking to see if Abbie took her other phone. She had one her father didn't know about."

When she couldn't find it, Wanda breathed a little easier. She wasn't ready to accuse Carson outright, but she knew who must have sent Delaney, and probably wanted Robbo and Thea permanently out of the way. Abbie was probably safe enough for a bit. Carson wouldn't want her dead.

"Do you know the number?"

"She did tell me, but I can't be sure I heard it right. However, she said she tried to ring me, so it might show up there ...if someone found my phone."

"Found where?" Thatcher demanded.

"You will need to ask Kelso," Wanda told him.

"Okay," Thatcher accepted that, but asked, "Perhaps you can explain why there has been a full scale look out for you for the past two days?"

"Obviously, because they couldn't contact me, and I didn't know to contact you."

Her statement was met with a faint shrug, as if he wasn't going to persist with trying to get a direct answer. Thatcher turned his attention to his colleagues. "When the forensic team arrives, I want photographs of each room, fingerprints, the works. In the morning we can quiz the neighbours."

More paramedics came in and they checked the two, still unconscious raiders, who were now restrained.

"What happened to them?" was the first question.

"I took exception to that one shoving a gun in my face, and I was trying to get to Abbie Carson, but that one had Thea and was in my way. They will probably come to, in another half an hour. Neither of them expected trouble from me."

Now that things had settled down, Wanda took out her task force ID and put the lanyard around her neck. Thatcher, moved closer and lifted the laminates for a look.

"So, what was your interest here? Are the two victims part of your investigation?"

"Peripheral, I think. But we have been after Mickey Delaney for obvious reasons. He shouldn't have been let out, and he is a prominent part of our activities. Kelso, who as you may be aware is also part of the task force, is also looking into Delaney's other activities – such as his relationship with Jeremy Carson."

Wanda added, to herself, "And a raft of things he tried to foist culpability for off onto his wife."

The second ambulance was told where to take the two unconscious intruders, and Wanda waited for Thatcher's attention to go to overseeing their transfer to stretchers, to head to Robbo's room.

It didn't work, he was more alert than she hoped.

"Where are you going?"

She had hoped to find out if there was anything lying around that was related to his feud with Carson. "To check Robbo's room."

"No!" Thatcher said flatly. "Tell us what you might expect to find, and my men can look over the room after the forensic team have finished. You, can go and sit down and explain to me how you knew the man that ran out was Delaney, when – from the two who just left, they all had stockings over their faces."

"It was Delaney," Wanda said flatly. "Even though he has

done something to his face so the left side seems reddened, and he has put some fake black spider web tattoos on his hand.”

“Why are you so sure?” Thatcher insisted.

“Because earlier today, or it might have been yesterday, he was where I was and thought me easy meat. I’m not!”

Thatcher snorted softly. “Go on.”

“Well, before he ran like a rat, I asked if he wanted another lesson. He didn’t, it seems, even though he had looked about to launch himself at me. He threw Abbie at the fourth guy, and yanked out his knife.”

“What happened to it?”

“It flew over behind that chair,” Wanda pointed, and was pleased when the detective went over, found it and bagged it.”

“Whose blood? The man who was staying here?”

“Yes,” Wanda confirmed.

Wanda only had the sudden alertness and the stiffening posture of Thatcher to warn her of who had arrived.

Commander Britten, leader of the Atlas Task Force came directly to where she was seated, and announced, “As of right now, Wanda Davis, you are stood down from operational activities.”

All sorts of objections flashed through her mind, but she voiced none of them. He was her boss, and he had the power to send her home, arrest her, or whatever he felt was warranted.

“Fine, Sir,” she agreed, keeping her voice strictly neutral.

“David, get the first aid kit from my car and see to your partner’s injury.”

That David didn’t even look to see what the problem was, suggested that he had caught some flak about her and was doing ‘anger control’ on the Commander. He was back within minutes.

“Get that jacket off,” David told her. “It’s pretty ripped already.”

Wanda caught David’s eye, and saw he was giving her a ‘keep

your mouth shut' expression with his lips thin and tightly closed. She nodded, ever so slightly.

"What happened?"

"One of them had a gun. Well, two did but I removed one from my first victim. The thinner of the two who just left, is a bad shot. Mickey hadn't got the message yet, and thought he'd finish me. The gun guy missed us both."

"You were trying to get Delaney killed, were you?" Thatcher asked.

"I hadn't known that guy had a gun, and Mickey still has too many dirty secrets I want to learn. Besides, killing him is too good for him. I want him to suffer in prison for a very long time."

David hissed a warning at her to stop volunteering her comments. He quickly inserted, "How are you otherwise?"

"Over it! I'm not addled," she said, answering David's unspoken question.

"Do you remember anything since Wednesday night?"

"Just flashes, until Abbie found me."

David's lips thinned again, she sensed he had questions for her that he didn't want to ask just then.

"How is the arm?" Commander Britten asked David.

"It is a nasty and deep graze from a bullet. She ought to get a doctor to look at it and decide if she should have a dose of antibiotics."

Britten merely nodded and went to talk to Thatcher. Wanda tried to hear, but her left ear, the one Leo had punched, seemed not to pick up any sound. She rubbed her hand there, to see if it felt normal. David took it.

"You have a bruise the size of your fist there. What happened?"

Wanda shook her head slightly. She didn't want to mention Leo in front of the Commander. Well, not just then. He was going to ask her that anyway, odds on.

David sighed quietly, but gave her hand a brief squeeze

before standing up.

"Right," Commander Britten announced then. "See that Superintendent Kingley gets a full report on all you find here. We'll be off."

Walking out beside David, with the Commander following, Wanda tried not to feel like she was being arrested. She did, however, remove her task force ID from around her neck, and pocketed it.

She realised, as soon as they went outside into the early pre - daylight, that quite a crowd of neighbours had come to watch the activity, and amongst them was at least one TV news crew. David had a grip on her uninjured arm, and she wondered if he had been told to act like an escorting police officer. She tried to think the question at him, but while he gave no overt sign of receiving it, she felt a brief squeeze on her arm.

Okay, she decided, something was up. But what?

Martin heard the early news on the radio and couldn't believe his ears. Abbie Carson? Kidnapped? Checking the time, he turned on the TV for the early news program. He saw her photo flashed on the screen – it was from last year's school photos. He listened to the details but they didn't make sense. Why had Abbie been in Footscray?

Almost as soon as the item finished, his phone rang. He wasn't surprised to hear Annie, practically crying.

"They think she's being kept somewhere around here," Annie repeated what he had just heard, another illogical fact. "We've got to help look for her."

"We don't know where to start," Martin said, reasonably.

"They pinged her phone, and the locator said it was around here," Annie persisted.

"They'll not have her in the open."

"She might have dropped it – as a clue. It might help narrow the area. Oh! Do you think if I called Wanda, they'd let us help? We can get the scouts that go to our school to help too. I'll call Naomi."

"I'll go get a paper. There might be more info in there."

Martin quickly finished dressing and headed out, making sure to lock his house securely. He paid no particular attention to the white van parked near the milk bar, as he assumed it was doing deliveries.

Abbie's photo was on the front page, along with one of her mother. Carson, he noticed with a faint smirk, wasn't. He was reading the article, still wondering how Abbie had ended up in Footscray, where she was reportedly taken from. Last he'd heard, via the grapevine at school, was that she had gone to visit relatives in NSW, and that was why she wasn't at school.

Well, that was what Annie's friend Karen had heard from her aunt, their home room teacher.

The van went past him, as he folded the paper so he could jog back home. He stopped when his phone rang again.

"Martin? I can't get Wanda. I forgot she was missing too, and doesn't have her phone. Can you ring David?"

"Yeah, okay."

"Tell him that Naomi, Karen and six or seven other scouts want to help."

"Okay. Hang up!"

David answered quickly. "Oh, Martin. What can I do for you?"

"Annie and I heard about Abbie being abducted and want to help. So do some of the scouts. Is Wanda back yet?"

"Just a moment," David requested.

Martin assumed the phone had been covered. He must be with others. Then he came back on the line. "Who's coordinating your group?"

"It was Annie's idea," Martin told him.

"I will give Kelly a call, and ring you back," David promised.

Martin didn't have to wait long for the reply. David told him, "Kelly will ring her. He's suggested the scouts could help the SES with a line search in Riverpark. They think that is where her phone is located. However, the thing went dead."

"Have you heard from Wanda? Annie's worried about her too."

David went silent again.

"David?"

"I'm here. Yes, she turned up, but I can't let you talk to her."

"Are you helping to find Abbie?" Martin wondered what the trouble was with his partner.

"No. That's for the local police. I've got our original job to finish. Look, I've got to get back to a meeting."

Martin took the hint, but he was disappointed that they couldn't help. David was right though. He had come to

Australia for a reason, and they would be expected to concentrate on that.

He called Annie and passed on the gist of the information. Finally, he said, "I'm near the park now. I'll hang around."

He saw all the police cars as he turned the corner. As he approached them, he heard his name called. On turning towards the sound, he saw DC Kelly gesturing to him.

"Martin, just the person to help us. Do you know if Abbie has any friends living near here?"

"Her main friends are Gail, Helen and Claire. Jackie too, before she got moved out," Martin said at once. "If you think she'd be with them, I don't know how without their parents knowing."

"We'll check them out. Can you give surnames and addresses?"

Names were easier, but he only had a rough idea of where they lived, but Kelly said it gave him something to work on.

"Why are you asking about them? Do you think Abbie staged this herself?"

"No, we are just covering all bases. Carson said his daughter has been going through a rebellious phase. We have an eyewitness to the abduction, but we are hoping she might have got herself free and headed home."

"But she hasn't, obviously. The news said her phone was somewhere in this area. Which doesn't make sense since I heard she had gone north to visit relatives."

"Apparently, Abbie and her mother came back yesterday and were staying the night in town," Kelly revealed.

"Well, how did she get to Footscray then? Did they take her there first?"

"No, it seems she headed there with some friend she had made while doing community service. She went to where a couple, who claim to be her siblings, were staying."

To Martin, the facts still didn't add up. "Was that friend Wanda?"

"I'm not at liberty to say. Now, your friend and the scouts

will be arriving at half past seven. They'll be working with the SES crew in a line search. You'd best head over there."

As he headed towards the SES caravan and a number of orange clad people, he wished Kelly could have said more. He also wondered why Kelly had clammed up when he mentioned Wanda.

What had she been doing? Something illegal? He refused to believe that she would be involved in hurting Abbie, or abducting her. Though the news did mention a woman staying there, in addition to the two who he assumed were the ones claiming kinship to Abbie.

Annie flew from her Dad's car as soon as he stopped to let her out. She had the pup with her and Martin grinned. He hoped the little flea brain had learnt something from the police dog the other week. Or lived up to its habit of finding things. It seemed to think this was a big game. It was frisking along as it trotted to keep up with Annie.

The SES volunteers, in their bright orange overalls, were being briefed by one of the police officers, and several TV vans were setting up.

"They're like vultures," Annie grumbled. "It's like they think we are looking for a body, not a phone. Who'd want to abduct her anyway?"

Martin only said, "We don't have enough information." Though he had been wondering that himself. The obvious answer was the two who wanted to get Carson's attention, but they hadn't been the ones to snatch Abbie away.

He had to turn his head to listen to the instructions. The scouts, including Annie and himself, were to be intermixed with the SES people and spaced out in a line. He intended to make sure he was next to Annie. They were to start moving around the outer edge of the park, and when they reached the starting point, to regroup and do a circuit further in.

Lucky-pup was having a high time, shoving her nose under low bushes and getting her lead tangled. Martin took it from Annie when she admitted her hand was sore from keeping the eager pup back from disappearing completely.

"Oh, no, mutt!" he warned the dog. "You leave the baby ducks alone." He assumed that was why she started barking, but when he tried to pull her back from under the bushes screening the pond, she wouldn't budge. He tried to drag her...

"No! You'll strangle her," Annie contested. "She might have found something."

The SES woman next to them suggested, "Have a look, lad."

Giving the lead to Annie, and a scowl in the direction of the pup, Martin crouched to look into the bush. He pulled out a black glove and held it up. The woman took out a plastic bag sealed the glove in it and made a notation in texta of where it was found.

Annie patted her ecstatic pup, who was ready to go on again. Martin was ready to swear the pup was actually strutting.

They continued for another fifteen minutes, and were behind the back of the shopping centre, when Lucky-pup began to play up again. This time, there was a lot of good natured grinning along the line and comments of, "What has she found this time?"

Martin was elected to check under the low bush. This time he didn't pull out the item.

"We might have found the phone."

The same woman as before pulled out another bag to use to pick it up, and word was passed along the line to the team leader. He came trotting up, but told the line to stay in place.

Annie edged around so she could look at the phone. It wasn't like the one she had seen Abbie use that night at her place. This was a fold-up one. She told the woman as much, as the team leader called the find in. DC Kelly and his partner, someone Martin didn't know, came to examine the find. The stranger used his phone to request information about the type of phone Carson's daughter had.

Annie heard and said, "I thought she had a Samsung."

"Nah, her father changed it. Scrubbed all the names off the old one and the SIM card," Martin told her. Kelly took the bagged phone as his partner said, "Her father says she has a Nokia. This is an Oppo," Kelly said, after examining it through the plastic.

There was a murmur of disappointment, but Annie picked up Lucky-pup for a well-done cuddle. "That's what we are looking for, Lucky. See if you can find another, okay?"

The pup wriggled and licked her. Annie put her down and used her sleeve to wipe her face.

The order was given to move forward again, but Kelly said, "You two, stick around a moment. You can rejoin the line in a bit." He gestured them over to the police car where he pulled out a pair of latex gloves and put them on. Then, using his pen as a stylus, pressed the 'on' button of the phone. He nodded when it didn't show an empty battery.

"Why do you need us?" Martin asked.

"Well, just between you and me, your friend Abbie got herself a new phone. The one Carson got for her was left behind at the place where she went."

"Then how did you get the new number or whatever you needed to see where the phone was?" Annie asked.

Kelly just tapped his nose, then grinned. "She called her supposed siblings and it was found on one of their phones."

"So they didn't take her from the hotel?" Martin asked.

"I don't know details," Kelly claimed, and Martin wondered if that was his way of not telling them too much. Kelly went on, "And I hope that you will keep very quiet about any suppositions that you make."

His tone was serious. "Now, I need to check if I can find the number this phone has, or see if either of you recognise any numbers on it."

"Oh!" Annie exclaimed. "So if we do, this is the phone we were looking for."

Kelly nodded and accessed the phonebook function first. "Good thing she didn't put a password on it. Okay, this looks like Greek to me."

"Let me look" Martin asked. When he did, he said, "She has used Greek letters for initials. Annie, what Greek letters do you know?"

"Some. They get used in maths and science a bit."

Annie glanced down the cryptic list, looking at the letters and phone numbers as Kelly scrolled down. "Stop. Go back up. That one. That's my phone number."

Martin looked over her shoulder. Further down, he said, "That's Carson's landline, and that one! It's Wanda's number."

"Yes, it is!" Annie grinned. "So it is Abbie's! Then she must be around here somewhere."

"Seems like she came back here. Which leads to the interesting questions of how and why," Kelly mused. "Hang around, I need to report to the Super."

He moved away, but they still heard parts of what he said. He ended with a series of 'Yes, Sirs'.

Martin exchanged looks with Annie. As Kelly strode off to talk to the SES control post. They were surprised when the line of searchers were directed to keep going. He returned and remarked, "Good work! You have allowed us to confirm that she is likely around here. Do you want to go back to join in looking? In case she dropped anything else?"

"Or they dumped her," Martin said without thinking. Annie made a strangled sound, and lifted Lucky-pup up for a cuddle.

"That's not likely," Kelly assured her. "Carson had a ransom demand pushed under his door. So, what do you want to do?"

"Have the police looked near the back of the shops?" Martin asked. Kelly nodded. He went on, "Well, I thought we could try the mutt out sniffing there. She's on a hat trick."

"I don't think there is any reason to stop you. So you try that and call if you find anything."

"I do hope Abbie's okay," Annie said as they walked towards the back of the shops, with Lucky-pup zig-zagging like a scent vacuum cleaner. "Do you think there's anything else to find?"

Martin shrugged. "At least we are doing something to try and help. Did you see the Hell's Angels just watching from their bikes?"

"No. but maybe they weren't allowed to help."

"True. The powers know that scouts have sense."

"You really don't like those three, do you?"

"No."

"Why?"

"It's not important. They're just full of themselves."

Annie stopped as her dog sniffed at an empty beer can. "That's not a phone, Lucky-pup."

"What did you call that overgrown rat? Lollipop?" Gail Conte's spiteful voice asked as she braked her bike to a stop just ahead of them. Clare and Helen stopped just past her.

"Are you helping to look for Abbie too?" Annie asked, ignoring the nasty comment.

"Abbie's probably got what she asked for," Gail said dismissively. "Like she tried with Tory. She'll be lucky if they find her alive, the little tramp."

"So you've dropped her now," Martin challenged, aware that Annie was trying not to show how upset she was by the comment.

"Do you know what this little stunt of hers caused?" Gail, spat. "My father didn't like having the police knock on our door to see if she was staying there. He said, rich bitches like her are nothing but trouble. And since she decided to get

stingy with her money, I'm not inclined to care." She turned to
her cronies. "Come on you two, let's get a drink and come back
to watch more of the entertainment."

"Absolute bitches!" Annie exploded, and she began to urge her dog to continue so no one would see she was crying.

"You don't usually let them get to you," Martin commented after a while.

"Sorry. I'm just worried."

"How about we cut through the storage place and get something to eat and drink too? I didn't get breakfast."

"I couldn't face breakfast," Annie admitted. "But I feel if we do that we are as bad as those bitches."

"Well, as least we have helped. We found the phone."

"Lucky-pup found it."

"Lollipop indeed!" Martin snorted. "Lucky is right. Come on, there's a laneway just up here. It saves going all the way around."

They turned onto the concrete path from the gravelled one they'd been on. Lucky-pup was still avidly sniffing all the new smells.

"There's a fence in the way," Annie said, dismayed.

"Nah, it's a gate, but never locked," Martin assured her. He jogged forward and shoved it open.

"Wait a sec, will you?" Annie called. "Can you hold Lucky's leash while a get a stone from my shoe?"

Martin returned and was reaching for the lead just as the dog took off. "Rotten little beast!" he muttered as he dived for the trailing leash. The little dog, finding itself free, ran faster.

Only when Lucky stopped to leave a deposit near the gate, did Martin manage to plant his foot on the lead. "You don't happen to have a bag for the dog poo do you?"

Annie finished retying her shoe and stood up, checking the pockets in her jacket. "You're in luck!" She handed it to Martin.

"It's your dog!"

"You asked for the bag, so it's your turn!"

With a mock scowl, Martin bagged the mess, still keeping a foot on the leash. "There's a bin out in the main street. She'd better not try doing another dump."

Lucky-pup wasn't paying attention. Now she was sniffing under the open gate, trying to dig a hole in the concrete with her front paws. "What's with you and small places, dog?"

"There's something between the gate and the wall," Annie said. "I saw something bright green."

Martin walked through the gate, which opened towards the street, and began to close it. The little dog dived into the space as soon as it was big enough for her, and dragging Marin's arm that way. Annie finished pushing the gate closed and gasped.

"What?" Martin asked.

"Abbie has sport shoes like that!"

"So do umpteem thousand people who can afford Nikes." He watched the dog half drag, half carry it to Annie.

One touch was all it took, even if the look hadn't been enough. Annie felt herself experiencing something totally foreign to herself. She let the image take hold, saw a mean looking man chucking the shoe into the laneway, and as the image unwound backwards, saw another horrid looking man wrenching the shoe off a foot, and the sharp sense of terror, knowing it was Abbie's.

Martin shook her out of the trance, and she gulped.

"Oh, gods! It is Abbie's, she was rolled up in a blanket somewhere. Some guy with a squashed looking face took her shoe off and another guy threw it somewhere."

"Can you tell where they were?"

"No...but I think the man that threw the shoe, came from that way. From the street. And the first man had a dark stain on his hand."

"And you are sure it's Abbie's shoe?"

Annie nodded. "It's the one I had to wear home that day at the start of term. It has orthopaedic foot inserts in it."

Martin felt inside, and then pulled out his phone to dial Kelly.

Within five minutes, a pair of uniformed police walked in from the street to meet them. Annie was holding Lucky-pup to stop her playing with the shoe, and as a distraction to stop herself feeling ill. She was happy to let Martin explain their find.

They listened carefully and asked, "And you are sure it belongs to Abbie Carson, Miss..."

"Annie. Yes. Mr Gill thought it clever to make us exchange shoes for the night after Abbie and I had a bit of an argument."

"It wasn't an argument," Martin contested, arguing with Annie. To the officers he said, "Annie was on the end of some petty bullying, as she was new to the school."

"So yes, I know it is hers. It's got an orthopaedic insole. You can check with her dad."

"We'll do that. DC Kelly is on his way around, and he wants a word."

"Lucky-pup can tell him how she found it," Annie said, cuddling the pup. "She has been right clever this morning."

Martin asked, "Is it okay if we wait in the street? I want to nick around to the nearest bin."

The officers smiled, and gestured them off. At the street, Martin said to Annie, "Wait here. I won't be long."

Annie decided to move just into the street, around to the front of the storage unit that bordered the lane. The cool breeze had begun to gust and tunnel along the lane and was making her feel cold. She leant against the rollup door.

Another vision hit her. She felt as if she had just suddenly stood up, and something had caused her heart to pound faster. She looked around, as the source of the alarm seemed so near. Then, as time rewound, she felt she was kneeling down, lifting a piece of broken concrete, like the piece near her feet. Then a man's face, close up, fiddling with...something, and then seeming to walk right through her with a box that somehow she knew was clanking slightly. The face seemed vaguely familiar.

"Annie?" DC Kelly called.

Annie jumped and turned around. "Oh, sorry. I was keeping out of the wind. Martin will be back in a sec."

"So I see. I hear that your clever dog found another clue."

"Yeah."

"And you are sure it is Abbie's?"

Annie nodded.

"You looked a bit ill, just then."

"It's nothing."

"She got a flash off the shoe," Martin said, coming up. He shrugged as Annie glared at him.

"I see." Kelly looked concerned, not sceptical. "Feel up to telling me about it?"

"You won't make me swear to it?"

"No. This is right off the record."

Annie tried her best to recall the details and the feelings and put them into words. Kelly didn't try to interrupt. "And just then, I leant against the roller door and saw..." She described that vision. "But I don't know why that one was so strong if the person was just putting stuff in there to store. It is hardly a thing for great emotion. I think he was somehow furtive."

"Well, I might just go get a list of people who have hired these units. However, take your mind back to the two men involved with the shoe, could you recognise them if you saw them?"

"One maybe. His face was reddened on one side, like a scald scar. And his hand was black. It was a bit like the guy I saw at school, but this guy was bigger and more solid looking."

"Excellent," Kelly praised them. "Let's just go for a walk along here to see if your clever dog smells anything else.”

“Why haven’t you brought in a proper police dog?” Annie asked.

“The dog squad are all busy out west looking for a missing hiker,” Kelly said with a trace of frustration.

Episode 17

Setting a Trap

Chapter 1

They entered the police building via the police garage, and went up to where Commander Britten had been given the use of an office. There, the first thing he did was point Wanda to a seat and arrange for a police doctor to come up to look her over. He didn't delay any longer than that to begin his interrogation.

"Right! Tuesday night. What happened?" He was expecting instant compliance. "David, take notes. Go on!"

"When I went out the back, to avoid being seen by Gilroy, I went around the house and was heading towards Fred's car —"

"That's Kelso's driver," David inserted as he wrote quickly.

Wanda went on to give all the facts until Britten stopped her at the point where she was tied up in the house.

Then he really grilled her, questioning motives, impressions, and her actions.

"I'm told, you could have got yourself free," Britten challenged. "Why didn't you?"

"I had recognised the bloke who carried me off," Wanda admitted. "It gave me an in with the local branch of The Family."

"An in? They might have killed you, woman or not!"

"No. Leo and Stephan owed me a big favour."

Britten moved around to his desk and flicked through a neat pile of manilla folders. "I don't recall those names," he remarked, thoughtfully.

"They aren't local," Wanda told him. "I know them from Austria, five years ago." Part of the reason for her inclusion in the task force was her connection to The Family.

"I see. Are they your relatives?"

"Uncles, yes. There were three of them, but I never met Nikolai then. I have now."

David looked up. "It's definitely Gilroy?"

"Yes, and he seems to be an up and coming 'Father', but once I'd shocked them by a) calling them by name, and b) reminding two of them that they owed me, and how they'd failed to help their sister, Gilroy recalled that women in the family were meant to be cherished. Then, since I didn't immediately run off when he ordered me untied, they took it that I wasn't averse to acting outside the Task Force mandate."

"As indeed you test the limits," Britten stated. "Could you have left after that?"

Wanda knew that he would know if she lied. If she could justify her actions, the truth would be better. Possibly he had quizzed David too.

"Leo Tatarovich has a shorter fuse than the others. He gave me a sample of what he'd do if I ran back to you. But, yes, I could have left during the night."

"So, why didn't you?"

"They were going to get Mickey out, because he claimed to have the missing specs from the prototype. His message to them was, effectively, 'Get me out and I will take you to them.'"

Britten decided to tell her, "We had Kemple under observation. He was in a café by himself for several hours. Then a big man came and sat at his table...."

The description of the man was Leo, and she confirmed it.

"He went out the back door," Britten continued. "However, we were able to find out where he went."

"Do you have the specs?" Wanda blurted, and this time Britten's grim visage relaxed.

"Yes, and we are in the process of having some subtle errors introduced into the blue prints and other records."

"Where were they?"

"In a locker at Southern Cross Station. Kemple went to his PO Box in Kew. One of the staff recalled that he came in to collect a large letter. The CCTV footage confirmed it. We also found the taxi that took him into town. Footage from within the station showed him getting a locker and putting the envelope in it."

"What was also interesting was that we had a glimpse of Delaney there on Wednesday, but he, and those with him, were gone before we could get anyone there," David added.

"What time was that?" Wanda asked.

"About four-thirty."

Wanda nodded. It fit with what she recalled. "You didn't tell me about that when I rang you."

"I couldn't," David apologised. "They didn't want to risk you accidentally letting it slip."

His expression was bland. He obviously hadn't agreed.

"Delaney gave the uncles the slip just after that," Wanda said. "Uncle Leo was furious. Delaney had a locker key on him. Whoever processed him must have missed the significance. They only found a mess of clothes in there, but the unit may have been kept there later if had been at Kemple's garage when the police went there."

"So," Britten concluded, "Delaney must have told Kemple to get a different locker for the envelope. He was probably laughing the whole time those others were looking."

"Only, the joke's on him," David clarified. He changed topics. "Did you get any hint of this Carson business from Delaney?"

Wanda noticeably paled. "No hint of last night's events, but I reckon he put the squeeze on Carson for money to get away. Carson probably made the favour to help get his daughter, part of his agreeing to pay up."

Britten interrupted. "Are you saying that Carson had Delaney abduct his own daughter?"

His voice seemed to thunder in the room. "Do you have any evidence to prove that?"

The statement had come out without her intending, but it fit with the myriad of impressions she had picked up.

"No," she was forced to admit. "Not that you can use."

"Was this related to something you got out of Delaney?" David asked. "That you didn't want to talk about?"

Wanda nodded, forcing herself to sit calmly, but she couldn't meet Britten's eyes.

"David, would you request Des Kingley to come up, if he is free."

Britten continued to stare at Wanda during the ten minute wait for the local police superintendent to arrive. The police doctor was with him but that didn't distract her from the queasy feeling in her gut. Britten and Kingley could have her arrested for the things she was going to have to admit. She couldn't hold back. It was very little help that she could sense David's empathy with her.

"Des," Britten greeted. "I thought you should be here for this. Mrs Martin?"

"I'm using Davis while I am here," Wanda muttered, as a delaying tactic. David was unwrapping the bandage he'd put on her arm and explaining to the doctor what he had done.

"Wanda has a theory that Delaney was doing a favour for Jeremy Carson, by abducting his daughter," Britten introduced.

That had Kingley's immediate and intense interest. "Kelso has been keeping me up to date," he admitted. "I have to agree that it does seem that Carson and Delaney do know each other." The observation was neutral.

Wanda looked at Kingley. Right then, he wasn't glowering

at her as Britten was, and talking helped block the pain in the arm from the fresh handling it was getting.

"You know I let myself be taken away by Leo Tatarovich?"

"That was the conclusion we came to. I've heard most of what you learned from Delaney, which I assume The Family also learned. You have more – that relates to recent police matters? You identified Delaney as the one who took Abbie Carson, even though he was disguised. Was there more?"

Wanda nodded. "I used hypnosis to get the info I did from Delaney. Yet I could tell, that even entranced, he was lying about some things. Leo, and the others, seemed to accept what he said as truth. Anyway, I could have rushed back then, but I'd not commented when Delaney tried to convince them he'd given the specs to Carson."

Kingley eyed her and skipped ahead to the time when they knew she had been in Carson's place. "Were you the one to open Carson's safe?"

Wanda nodded, then winced as the doctor gave her an injection close to where her arm was hurt. She heard him tell David it was both antibiotics and analgesic. She was glad when the new bandage was finally in place.

Chapter 2

"Did you look through the safe?" Kingley asked.

"No," Wanda said. "Gilroy did that, but I took the opportunity to look through some concealed cupboards. Obviously, I didn't find the envelope there. I did hope to find another thing. Abbie mentioned to me that her father had a copy of Gabriel Hartley's birth certificate in an envelope with her name on it. It had been in a plain box file marked 'family'. I found that box but not that envelope."

Kingley opened his mouth to challenge her on that, but she went on quickly, "I know it's proof of nothing and there could have been lots of reasons why it wasn't still there. However, Abbie also mentioned the box had been stuffed with family documents – envelopes and papers, it wasn't when I saw it. The amount of stuff in those cupboards didn't tally with Abbie's observation either. I also believe that if you can get co-operation from Robbo and Thea, they'll say the same."

Wanda paused, this time Kingley merely said, "Back to Delaney."

"Yes. He and Carson have known each other for a very long time. Twenty years or more. He first knew Carson as Jacob Hillier. He met when Hillier tried to interest Delaney in a Horse Racing Speculation System. One where you pay a thousand dollars up front to get the benefit of a number of hot prospects each week. Of course their blurb showed consistently more winners than losers. Mickey ended up touting the program for Hillier and taking some of the profits – until Hillier had to duck out of sight."

Kingley was jotting something down in a notepad, possibly questions. He looked up and Wanda continued, "Nearly twenty years ago, a number of years after the other scam folded, Carson, as Hillier was now known, happened to run into Delaney – maybe not by accident. Carson asked Delaney to collaborate on a long term investment project.”

David, listening to the sickening details, now understood why Wanda had not wanted to talk of it earlier. It was a plan, to deliberately and unscrupulously usurp the Hartley family fortune. To remove the original heirs, to create a new heir using Maude Hartley and then to remove her from the picture. Then, many years later, have the new heir’s father bring that heir to Maude’s trustees, and gain control of the money as the child’s father/guardian.

Britten was no longer glowering, and even Kingley was white faced.

“Carson was approached by the Department of Human Services yesterday. They were acting on behalf of the Hartley Trust, to look him over. We were asked to do a police check, which as I told you earlier, found nothing. This alters things.”

“I know it’s virtually hearsay,” Wanda admitted. “But there are points that fit with things that I picked up from Maude. They targeted her because of her outward handicap. Maude told me that ‘Mickey think stupid is deaf’. But a lot of people think, ‘simple is forgetful’. Maude thought she recognised Carson, but not by that name. And I am sure her memory is good – of times when she wasn’t being drug addled by Delaney.

“I believe she knew Carson, to some degree, a long time ago – she said she called him Wally. He came to visit just after her parents died to express his condolences. The twins were conceived about then. They were both using each other. Maude wanted a child to carry on the Hartley name, and Carson wanted one he could control. Tyrell also thought he was familiar and didn’t know the name. So I believe that Carson (as Wally) must have worked at the Trustee Company and learnt about the family. He might have known of the trust set up for Maude’s little boy that died, and expected the same for the twin girls.”

Kingley sat contemplating for a while, his thoughts not revealed by movement or expression. “Very well, let’s take that as a hypothesis. How does that work into the present events and help us find Abbie Carson?"

"We know Delaney called Carson to warn him of his visitors," David put in. "We know he is intending to pay Delaney 50K. Likely for the services Wanda mentioned. Delaney was probably caught and jailed not long after Maude was committed, before he was paid, unless that was not to be until Carson had his hands on the money."

"Delaney was jailed about two months after the committal," Kingley confirmed.

Wanda began again, "Abbie said that she and her father have an appointment with the Hartley Trustees, today or tomorrow. She thinks her father is up to something dishonest, and she doesn't want any part of it. Her running off again, wasn't in Carson's plans. He needs to maintain his outward untarnished reputation. I think he would have been angry when Robbo called him to taunt him about losing something and I think he has a way that he used to track Abbie's phone to Footscray. I think he devised a plan to achieve a number of desirable outcomes in one move."

Wanda paused to gauge the reaction of the two high ranked policemen, one American, one Australian. She went on, "One, he pays back Mickey for the visitors. Two, if Abbie is abducted and a ransom demanded as untraceable cash, he has a blatant reason for withdrawing that much money from his bank. A reason the Department of Human Services and the Hartley Lawyers couldn't fault. He might even think the Hartley Foundation might reimburse him when Abbie is safely back and confirmed as heir. Lastly, it is a rather draconian way of telling his rebellious daughter, that 'Daddy knows best'."

"You have an extremely devious mind," Kingley accused her. "The problem is, if you are right, how do we prove it?"

"Well, I've had some thoughts about that," David spoke into the silence. "Some ways to catch Carson out, capture Delaney, and I don't think he will go anywhere near a ransom drop, and catch the contacts wanting the specs and perhaps some of the family too."

"I hope it includes finding Abbie Carson very quickly," Kingley said directly.

"What's the latest on the search?" Wanda asked. She knew that David had received a call from Martin in the car and mentioned that he, Annie and the scouts had wanted to help search locally. She'd not heard any more.

Kingley used his phone to request an update from someone. He told the group, "We found her phone, the one you mentioned that Carson didn't know about. And found one of her shoes. DC Kelly requested a list of people renting the storage units near the park. We've applied for a warrant to search one rented by an R. Mainwright."

"No! That's a ruse," Wanda blurted.

"Explain your thoughts," Kingley directed.

"Another way Carson could benefit is to throw suspicion on the two who are claiming he is their defaulting father. I don't believe they knew Mickey Delaney, or told anyone to come and get Abbie. The worst they did was to encourage her to come to them, and perhaps encouraged the idea of revolt against her father. They would be better off keeping her close and safe, and grateful, don't you think?"

"A good point. Unfortunately, Robbo won't be in any condition to be questioned for a while."

"Thea would be," Wanda pointed out.

"We will definitely need to talk to them about Carson," Kingley agreed. "Okay, David, what was your plan?"

Chapter 3

When his phone vibrated, Delaney answered it quickly. "Yeah, what? It's you...never you mind where she is, mate. Just be the worried Daddy. How are you planning to get me my money?"

Mickey wasn't worried when Carson said, there would be a ransom note with his morning paper, but he scowled as Carson told him to send a message saying to have the money in a case and when and where to put it, with the caveat, 'No police'.

"You're mad if you think I will pick it up."

Carson's next words soothed him. "Of course not. If no one shows, they'll bring the money back here I'll have it, and can get it to you when things cool down."

"I've a better idea. I come and get it while the attention is elsewhere. Have some in the case - tell them the ransom is 25K, and have the rest at your place. I know damn well you have stashes and I bet you have 25K easy! Then as you said, if no one shows, and the money goes back to you, you can give me the rest of what you owe me."

"Yes, that will work. In spite of your trying to ruin everything by knifing that punk. Not that I care if he dies. If asked, I will imply they had accomplices. They had the punk girl and another woman taken to the city for questioning. That woman was one of my unpleasant guests."

"That woman is unnatural," Mickey told him. "I'd like to see her in hell for this."

"As would I. However, I had a thought – to get Lonny to arrange bail for her as soon as she's finished being questioned. She won't be at the city lodgings for very long."

"I'll get someone to meet her, if the bail guy will bring her to him. I want her. Don't want her testifying against me."

65

"Get her to open my safe again," Carson suggested. "I didn't believe how easily she did it. My police friend admitted she was a former safecracker. And I don't think her task force bosses fully trust her. I was told, in confidence that her bosses have revoked all privileges and her operational status. They don't believe she was defending my poor little girl, rather they think she was running interference. Anyway, once she has the safe open, you don't need her. Leave her there for the police to find when I get back home. I doubt they will believe anything she says."

"And I have the perfect patsy to be the drop receiver." Micky chuckled. "I have a score to settle with a mate's kid. Know just how to fix him so he will go for the bundle and keep his mouth shut and if he welshes, or gets caught, no matter. He'll be put in jail for sure."

Crane's knock came when it was just starting to get light. Mickey checked through the back peep hole before opening up.

"Come quickly," Crane warned. "The cops are everywhere. I have a plain white van. Word is out on the radio and telly about the snatch. Somehow they know we are around here."

"Put her in first," Mickey said quickly. "We can put some of the builder's rubbish in next, as if we are clearing the place for the refit."

They worked with purpose, Mickey remembering to get the tool kit he had snatched from the boot of the BMW.

Moving without apparent haste, Crane drove the van towards Kemple's house, parking at the nearby milkbar, where they would not seem suspicious.

Mickey sent Crane to get the morning paper, while he turned on the radio for the morning news. He had to silence Crane to hear the details. Carson would be pleased. As he had said, the punks were in for questioning, as was the woman, and would likely be charged. None of the three were talking. It made him chuckle until he saw a figure he recognised.

What was Kemple's kid doing at the milk bar this early? Had he decided to whack off school today? Of all days? Mickey hid his face in the paper – what luck!

"Crane, drive off casually. Go back the way we came until I tell you to stop."

If Kemple's kid was out and about, he would go to his place and wait. Fix him, and blame that on his old man, then stash the girl in his garage and be away.

Then, he'd use Crane's phone to call Carson's house and give the message about the ransom. No one would recognise his voice at the moment. He could get some of his own back on the kid in the meantime. It would be tomorrow at least before Carson got the money.

When Martin hadn't returned to his home when Delaney expected, he had Crane drive around the park where the news had mentioned a search.

"Is that him, Mickey?" Crane pointed to group of young people near those in SES orange.

"Yes he's one of them. Get back to Kemple's place. We'll have time to ditch the freight in the back – "

Mickey stopped to think. "No, go via the hardware place first – we'd best get a new lock in case the other one was wrecked."

Crane did as directed, being the one to go into the shop. Then, when they returned to Kemple's place he backed the van into the drive, and down nearly to the garage. They waited a few minutes before getting out, but there was no indication of any interest from the neighbours.

Crane went to the front door, as if there for a legitimate reason, but there was no answer. He shrugged and went around to the rear of the house. By then, Delaney had already cut the lock that was on the side door of the garage, with bolt cutters that had been in the toolbox from the Mercedes.

"Help me with that carpet," he ordered, urging haste.

Threats of injury silenced the whimpering as they carried Abbie wrapped in a thick blanket.

Mickey managed to free a hand to turn on the light so he could see where to put the girl. He chuckled. Someone had gone over the place after he had to leave, tidied it and added more junk in boxes. Even though he didn't care, he put the girl down carefully, and pulled the stocking back over his head when he uncovered the girl's head. He savoured the look of terror in her eyes as he took out his knife and brought it near her face.

"You be very, very still," he warned, as he poked the knife through the tape across her mouth where her lips were. He had a bottle of water, one that had been left in a fridge in the abandoned Chinese shop, and a straw that he had picked up and wiped the dirt off.

"Have a drink," he invited, enjoying the look of disgust that preceded the desperate slurping. Too bad he didn't have anything to put in it to knock her out, but he still had more chloroform.

Five minutes later, the girl was out again and he went out and locked the door. Now for the next part of his plan.

"We need new wheels," Delaney told Crane. "Drive into the city a bit."

Delaney had his eyes out for a likely vehicle, and when he saw the ex post office van, he said, "That one."

Within moments, Mickey was in it and had the engine running. He drove around the next corner after Crane, and followed to a quiet street where, the van stopped and Crane had the licence plates off the first van, ready to swap them with those of the newly stolen van. They were back in Bellfield as the searchers were dispersing. He had Crane drive around as he scanned the crowd for Martin Kemple. He spotted him coming back from the direction of the shops, but he was with a girl. That was a complication.

"Follow them well back," Delaney directed. The initial slow speed wasn't a problem because people were walking everywhere, back to cars and across the road.

At the corner of Martin's street, the girl went on and Delaney gestured for Crane to turn left and drive to just past Kemple's place. As soon as Martin had turned into his drive, Delaney was out, trotting on the nature strip to catch up to him before he went inside.

They actually walked past all the units without Lucky-pup doing any more than sniffing enthusiastically. Martin decided that Kelly was thinking the units would be a place where someone might stash a prisoner. He didn't want to say so, but hoped that if Abbie was in one, the little mutt would smell her and react. Perhaps that had been Kelly's thought too.

Kelly was called back to the SES post, but he said, "You've both been a great help. Could you also let the scouts know their help was appreciated?"

"Alright," Annie promised.

Watching Kelly drive off, Martin suggested, "Let's get that drink and food, huh?"

The searchers were dispersing by the time Martin and Annie finished their late breakfast. They saw the two media vans packing up.

"We might as well go home," Martin decided. He had enjoyed spending time with Annie, even under the circumstances.

"It's back to being helpless," Annie agreed. "I don't know how finding that stuff is going to help."

"I reckon Kelly knows more than he's letting on. Maybe what we found will provoke ideas."

"He said there'd been a ransom note, didn't he?"

"He did. I wonder if Carson's going to pay up?"

"He'd have to, surely," Annie turned to look at Martin.

"Well, he can afford to, even if he won't be happy about it."

"It's not Abbie's fault," Annie protested.

"I heard someone say that she left the hotel in town under her own steam," Martin told her. "Left herself open to trouble. She could have been attacked and left for dead. A ransom means she's alive."

"But why pick her? If it was just anyone doing it? Surely whoever did it had to have known who it was?"

"The news this morning said something that made me think of those two we met at school."

"Yeah, maybe," Annie said. "But weren't they arrested?"

"Hmmm. They may have had accomplices. Want me to walk you back home?"

"Maybe part of the way," Annie decided, feeling particularly vulnerable right then.

Martin was having pleasant thoughts as he went up his street. In spite of his concern for Abbie, he had really enjoyed being with Annie that morning. It seemed like it had been a long time since he'd had any kind of friend.

He had forgotten the warning that he needed to be alert, so when he felt the arm suddenly pinion him, and a hand cover his mouth, he thought it was his father. However, when he kicked out with his booted foot, the curses were unfamiliar.

"I've a very sharp knife, boy. You cause trouble and you will be in two pieces."

The voice was muffled, but Martin had the horrible feeling he knew who it was.

"Now, you just drop whatever you are carrying and come with me to the van up ahead."

The van's rear door opened, and Martin heard, "Get in and sit down."

Martin did as he was told, hoping that somehow, Annie would come back and find what he'd dropped. Then his mind was too busy trying to figure a way out of this spot, not to mention why he was being targeted and if it had anything to do with Abbie.

Martin studied the stocking squashed face, when the van turned and sunlight came in through the van's front window. There was a patch of darker colour on the man's cheek. It reminded him of the man he'd seen at the school talking to his cousins at the start of term. He glanced at the man's hand, but they were gloved. If it wasn't Delaney, had it to do with drugs?

Martin's stomach lurched. *Was he being set up?*

The van stopped. Martin couldn't tell where, but the driver came through from the front, through the gap between the two seats. He too had his face covered.

The knife in the other man's hands emphasised the order to stand up and turn around and put his hands on the side of the van.

When he'd done that, he felt himself being frisked, and his wallet, keys, phone and the change from when he got the paper were taken from his pockets.

"Hands behind you."

Now Martin did try to struggle, but there were two of them and one of him in a confined space. His efforts only delayed the tape being wrapped around his wrists and across his mouth. The driver returned to the front seat and Martin was yanked around and pushed back onto the seat.

Martin watched his captor, hoping he would come in range of his still free feet. The man was watching him, only switching his gaze away for microseconds as his free hand searched in a toolbox for something. He finally felt and pulled out a piece of waste cloth. The man glanced at it, muttered, "That'll do," and then he moved back closer to his prisoner.

When he realised that the oily smelling rag was to be used as a blindfold, he tried to propel himself head first into the man. It didn't work. The man was solid, like Delaney, he realised as his eyes began to sting from the chemical residue on the rag. The smell began to give him a headache.

Chapter 5

With an apologetic glance at his wife, David outlined a plan worthy of their usual covert operation controller.

"As things stand, the two Mainwrights only know Wanda as a disgruntled type, resenting being charged for a minor thing and made to do community service.

"The Family think she is open to going behind the task force's back, and they know she was in prison in Austria and what for. The media know a woman was arrested with the Mainwrights and is being questioned about Abbie's abduction. Carson won't be feeling very kindly toward her for easily opening his safe. He will likely believe she is a crook too."

"A very believable character profile," Commander Britten agreed, his eyes, hawk-like on his female maverick team member.

"Okay, if we play it right," David went on, "we might be able to get The Family to help track down Delaney –"

"I'd add Kemple to that too," Kingsley suggested, and David nodded.

"Have them deliver him to us," David continued.

"To me," Wanda inserted. "They know I have a thing against him, and I might be able to blurt out something I overheard about where you suspect the envelope was put – the swifty he pulled on them and me."

"We have a tracker chip in the envelope," David elaborated. "So when it is passed on, we can follow the trail. Either, to get the Serbian group reps, or the people who can build another unit from the specs."

"I'd also keep those uncles of mine owing me favours," Wanda said. "I don't think you will be able to get enough proof on them to hold them."

"We can," Britten overruled. "They are wanted by Interpol, aren't they? Two agents are flying here now. So if you intend to use them, we need to move quickly. First, I am going to arrest you for complicity in the abduction of Abbie Carson. I've already stood you down for unsanctioned conduct and admitting to other illegal activities.

"You'll be taken to the cells. When the Mainwright woman is released by the doctor, she can join you. Talk to her and find out all you can. Nothing that she tells you, can be used by us but if we pin Carson down to the things you suggested, we can find evidence."

"Not strictly legal either," Wanda feigned disgruntlement.

"I'll call Martin and give him a message for his cousins to pass on. If the family gets in touch, can you convince them to help find Delaney?" David asked. "That place Carson mentioned for him to go has turned up nothing."

"What if they get info out of Kemple about the locker? Stephan or Leo could get in without needing Delaney."

"Then call in an IOU," David insisted. "Surely getting Delaney and helping Maude is worth it?"

"And proving Carson is behind the abduction," Wanda agreed.

David took out his phone and tried Martin's number. "His battery must be flat."

"Can I borrow that? Or do you have mine?" Wanda gestured to the phone. "Why don't you find Gilroy's landline?"

Kingley asked someone to find the number, but the reply came back that it was unlisted.

"Never mind," she said, pushing buttons of a number she recalled seeing. Questioning eyes watched her, as she waited for the phone to be answered.

"That you, uncle?" she asked, when it was.

"You promised me Delaney. I want the bastard. He abducted a 15 year old girl early this morning."

She listened to the speaker with a scowl on her face. "Yeah, but they haven't done more that ask asinine questions...yeah, I know you won't you bastard, but I don't need your help for that. They can't keep me here....she isn't just anywhere! I heard them say the kid's phone was located in the park, and a shoe near some storage unit. That means Delaney brought her back around Bellfield, probably because he knows the area so well.... I didn't think he'd given you what you wanted yet either...no, I don't. I'm on shaky ground with them, and they aren't telling me anything."

When she finally ended the call, saying, "You can call this number back and leave a message," she was grinning. She turned to Britten and Kingley and said, "I reckon I have motivated them."

"If we get Delaney, the supposed abductor, and keep it quiet, and while we have Theo and Robbo where they can't contact anyone," David organised his thoughts, "If Carson claims to get any more messages, we will know he's sending them to himself. He needs to pay off Delaney, to get him off his back. So if the abduction farce still goes on..."

Wanda's attention to the plan was interrupted by a call on David's phone. She felt his reaction and braced herself for bad news.

"It's Kelso, sir," David told Kingley, "They entered unit 17, the one purported to be hired by R. Mainwright. They found some potentially stolen valuables, objects and silverware, in a box. As well as another shoe like the one the kids found outside. No sign of Abbie Carson. But there was also water and tinned food in there."

"Carson's plan didn't allow for the police watchers around the park," Kingley guessed. "If the hypothetical story you told me is true."

"So that means, that Delaney was meant to take the girl there, to implicate the Mainwrights for robbery and abduction," Wanda predicted. "Bet the box of stuff is from Carson's house."

"So, what would Delaney do with a teenage prisoner on the spur of the moment," Kingley asked. "He'd have needed to drop whatever car he'd stolen and stay out of sight. Just a moment. I will have the locals check for nearby empty houses and shops."

When Kingley finished that call, he began to quiz David on the technicalities of his plan. Wanda found herself yawning and trying to hide the fact. She didn't succeed. "Do you want me to get a stretcher bed brought up?"

"No, I'm fine," Wanda forced herself to sound alert. She didn't see David's expression, or his nodding to Kingley.

"What say, you write a report of all you did from Tuesday evening to when we found you at the house in Footscray? Include your discoveries and thoughts about various people," Britten directed. "David, Des and I will work on the plan and let you know what you need to do."

"How will you tell me if I'm down in a dungeon?" Wanda asked sweetly.

"I'll pick up an ear receiver," David told her. "Will it be a problem in that ear? I could have it covered by a bandage then."

"Do it," Wanda told him. "I'll need to stay in the loop."

Wanda accepted the paper and pen from Commander Britten and began to write. She was listening to the conversation as David explained his idea. She tried not to yawn, but the impulse was getting harder to ignore. She closed her eyes, intending it to be just for a moment....

She woke with David shaking her gently, and realised she was lying on a stretcher bed with a blanket over her and a lumpy cushion for a pillow. She jerked upright, "How long was I asleep?"

"Most of the afternoon," David said, grinning at her. "Thea will be going to the holding cells soon. We want you to be there before her. So you are going to be formally charged, and taken there."

"Apart from talking to Thea, what do I have to do?"

"I'll fill you in later. I need to put the ear receiver in, before we go."

David had all he needed for that, and set about removing the bandage currently over her ear and after inserting the pea sized receiver, put a new adhesive dressing on.

"Are you going to test it?" Wanda asked.

"I did already," he assured her. "Are you feeling better now?"

"Yeah, I guess I needed to pass out for a bit."

"Ok. Let's get going."

Annie hadn't gone more than a quarter of the way towards her place when she began to need a toilet. She continued a bit further, hoping the feeling would pass, but it didn't. Considering how long it would take her to get home, or to go back to Martin's place, she decided to call Martin and see if she could use the toilet at his place. The phone went dead after two rings. She tried again, thinking he may have accidentally cut her off, as she'd done to people a time or two, but this time it didn't even ring, she got the 'this phone is switched off' message. It didn't worry her greatly, since she could ring his door bell when she got there. Lucky-pup certainly didn't mind the change in direction, although the poor little thing was tired now. She picked the dog up so she could walk faster.

An old van drove past her, but she had no reason to pay it any attention. Her mind was on her own urgent problem. She almost ran up to the front door, reaching out with her free hand for the doorbell. She heard it echo inside and waited. No one came. She tried again, thinking Martin might be indisposed, like she needed to be. After four tries, spaced a few minutes apart, she was getting even more desperate, and there was still no sound to indicate Martin was there.

Maybe he was out the back, she thought, and couldn't hear the bell. After all, he wouldn't be expecting her to come there. Tentatively, she walked down the drive. Lucky-pup wriggled and wanted down. She put her down and kept walking while the dog stopped to sniff and pull out of some low bushes a red and white bag she recognised. Martin had bought an extra hamburger to have later. She reached down and took the bag from her dog.

The sensation of fear almost made her sick. Martin! Someone had grabbed him and ...

Lucky-pup was straining towards the garage, and was barking urgently. Annie ran down and saw no way to open the big door, and recalled the side door from Martin telling her of the police raid there. A new padlock secured it. Was he in there?

Something had her dog's attention. She reached for the lock, and had the sensation of someone being carried in there. Martin?

Annie called his name, but the dog's barking covered any other sound.

"Shh, Lucky!" The dog seemed to understand.

"Martin? Are you in there?"

Although she listened hard, she couldn't tell if the vague scuffling was the wind in the trees or something inside.

Without stopping to think, she pulled out her phone and dialled the emergency operator.

When asked who she needed, she said, "Police. I need the police."

The next speaker asked her the nature of her problem, and her state of worry caused her to garble her answer. The operator urged her to calm down.

"It's my friend, Martin. I think something has happened to him. He should be at home, but no one answers and the bag with his lunch in was dropped in his driveway."

"When did you last see him?" came the question.

"Less than twenty minutes ago," she answered truthfully.

The woman thought she was hysterical, for she suggested, "He might have had to go out for something. There seemed little evidence of a crime."

"You have to help!"

"I will put you through to the police non-emergency line," the operator offered, and Annie thanked her out of habitual politeness.

She had to explain it all again, and still they tried to tell her she was worrying about nothing. Even mentioning the van she had remembered seeing, didn't help. They must think she had argued with her boyfriend and he'd gone off.

"I am not being hysterical," Annie insisted, forcing herself to sound calmer. "Could you please ask DC Kelly from Bellfield Station to call me - Annie Jamieson. I'll give you my number. Please tell him it is urgent."

The operator ended the call, but Annie really wasn't sure that they would do anything. Meanwhile, her urgent need was getting even worse, and she was feeling she couldn't wait, so she considered doing something she had never thought she would dare. She went behind the garage, where two trees grew thickly together, and no one could see her, and relieved herself.

She emerged when she heard a car drive up and stop sharply. Checking first, she was relieved to see a police car. Lucky-pup started barking again, this time at the side door of the garage.

The two officers were strangers to her, but one asked, "Are you Annie Jamieson?"

"Yes,"

"You reported, something happening to your friend."

"Yes."

"Tell us what happened."

She went through it for the third time, as Lucky-pup's barking became more frantic.

"And I think, whoever caused him to drop his lunch, put him in there."

"It's locked," the other noted. He had been looking around.

"How well do you know Martin Kemple?"

Annie knew she hadn't mentioned Martin's surname, and now realised Martin was known to them.

"We walk to and from school together," Annie said, "and today we were helping to look for a class mate – Abbie Carson."

Their attitude changed, subtly. Annie wasn't sure why, and hoped they weren't thinking Martin was involved in that.

The officer, whose badge had read 'Parnell', turned away from her and spoke into the radio she carried, asking for instructions. Finally, she turned back and repeated what Annie had heard. "Someone will be coming to get us into the garage. Why aren't you at school? Just because you wanted to help?"

"No. It's a teacher free day."

"Do your parents know what you were doing?"

"Yes. Dad dropped me off at the park this morning. Martin and I went there with a group of scouts, to help."

"What about now? Did you tell them you were going to be visiting Kemple?"

Annie felt herself flush scarlet, at the thought of having to admit what she had needed to do, and done. There was probably a law against it.

"I remembered something I had to tell him and he wasn't answering his phone."

Parnell's expression seemed like a prelude to a 'that wasn't a very smart thing to do' lecture.

Another car arrived, pulling up abruptly. Annie felt much relieved when she recognised Kelly jogging down the drive, pulling something from his pocket.

"Annie. I heard what you reported. It probably wasn't a smart thing to come here. I told Martin not to suggest it. Anyway, I still have the key he gave me yesterday."

Kelly hurried to the side door, and fiddled with the key and lock. Frowning, he gestured for one of the constables to keep Annie away, and the other to back him up. Annie glanced that way and saw Kelly had his gun out.

After a moment to gather himself, he kicked at the lock, and the wood around it shattered. He kicked harder, until he had room to get in, but he did so carefully, first turning on the light and listening. He and the constable went in, and they didn't immediately reappear. She heard someone talking on the radio. Moments later, the big door was opening up. Annie saw a wrapped bundle on the floor and tried to go to it, but was held back. It wasn't Martin, she could tell that. The person had bleached blond hair.

Episode 18

Counter Trap

<u>Chapter 1</u>

"Abbie?" she gasped, trying to get free. When Kelly gestured for her to approach, she felt her arm released.

"Is she alright?" Abbie asked Kelly, pleading for him to say 'yes'.

"Unconscious, from chloroform, judging by the smell on the blanket. We have an ambulance coming, but you can wait with her. She's stirring, so talk to her. I will see what I can find to cut her loose."

The unexpectedness of the discovery completely overwhelmed her thoughts of Martin's plight. Lucky-pup tried to lick Abbie's face, but obeyed the quiet order to stop, and simply crouched down and stared.

Annie's ears were listening for the ambulance, when she was surprised by Abbie trying to speak.

"You'll be okay," Annie told her. "They have gone to get something to cut the tape."

Tears of relief began leaking from Abbie's eyes. Annie reached over and gently wiped them away, then gave Abbie's shoulder a gentle squeeze.

Kelly returned with the sort of scissors found in little first aid kits. He spoke quietly to Abbie as he worked to cut the tape.

"Okay, this might hurt, but I am going to pull off the tape, okay?"

Abbie nodded a bit and tried to talk. When her hands were

free, she tried to pull on the tape on her mouth.

"You need to be careful," Kelly warned. "You've been bleeding a bit."

Abbie didn't quite rip it off, but succeeded in freeing her mouth anyway.

"Drink?" she tried to say.

Kelly looked at the bottle and straw and said, "Let's wait a few minutes for the paramedics to look you over. I can hear the ambulance now." He stood up and went to talk to the two constables. His voice was too quiet for Annie to hear, but one of the constables went to wait at the gate.

The ambulance arrived, and the paramedics came down the drive with the patient trolley. Annie was pulled out of the way, but she breathed easier when Kelly was told Abbie would be fine after some rest. He asked them to keep the patients head covered as they wheeled her to the ambulance, and to give no name for the victim until he got there. "You will be going to...?"

"Royal Melbourne," he was told.

"Okay. I don't want any publicity about your patient. Imply it's a male, found unconscious. Will you do that? It is quite important that the media are misled."

It all sounded so cloak and dagger, but Annie refrained from asking questions. Kelly was holding her arm as Abbie was wheeled along the drive, and from the contact, she vaguely sensed the reason. Still, she was startled when Kelly asked her, "Can I ask you to mention to no one that we found Abbie Carson?"

"Yes, but why?"

"Because finding her was a fluke," he admitted, "and we have an opportunity to catch the culprits. They didn't count on you. If we make the neighbours think it was Martin, or one of his less than desirable friends, it will give us reason to be watching the street. We might mislead the abductors into revealing themselves."

"But won't her parents want to know?"

Kelly's expression was unreadable. "We will let them know, but advise them against visiting her right away. So please, tell no one, not even your parents or Martin if he comes back."

"But that's what I originally called the police about," Annie blurted. "I think someone grabbed him."

Annie explained why she came back, and knowing that Kelly was aware of her talent, mentioned that too. His expression changed to a frown.

"I will have a call put out to look for him," Kelly promised. "And I will get you home. Will either of your parents be there?"

"No, but I'll be okay," Annie assured him. Now someone was believing her, she felt like bawling. "I can't understand why someone would take him."

"We will have to find out why. Come on. When you get home, make yourself a hot drink and have something to eat."

Annie found herself unsettled during the afternoon. She had her radio on to listen to the news, but heard nothing about Abbie, and wondered what the police were doing. It was frustrating to know some of it, but not the rest. That reminded her of the flashes she had received that day, and she went to write them down before she forgot all the details. She also added notes to earlier entries where she had learnt more about what had happened. The flash she'd had from Martin's lunch bag, had been strong, and she tried to see if she could recall more detail, but no. Martin had not seen who had grabbed him.

When her mother returned from work, it was a relief to have someone else to distract her. It was hard to pretend that her bad mood was worry about Abbie, who she knew to be safe, when she was really worried about Martin. When the evening news came on – the only mention was that the police were still seeking Abbie Carson, and waiting for her kidnappers to get in touch. A brief mention of one of the storage units being checked had her attention, but they announcer hadn't needed to say it gave no clues. They referred to three people being detained in Footscray at the house where Abbie had been taken from. They had a quick shot of two people being taken off in an ambulance – one walking, one on a stretcher, and another of a woman being taken to a police car – had that been Wanda? No names had been given. Over all it was the usual sort of non-information. And she knew it to be partly false, and couldn't say so. As for Martin, he probably didn't rate a mention even if the news media had found out about him. Maybe they would have more on the late news?

Having Naomi ring up was a welcome distraction, even though the conversation began about Abbie. However, Naomi had news. The scouts had permission to have the old house demolished, and her dad had managed to get the people to do it for them at no charge, by giving them permission to salvage any fittings and materials that could be reused or sold.

Naomi went on to say, "My dad has plans to get a lot of the materials for the new place donated as well, so that the Hartley Trust doesn't have to pay out as much. They already have given us the land and all."

"When will that happen?" Annie said, knowing her father was involved in the plans for the new building.

"Pretty soon, I think," Naomi said. "Dad said the police were okay with that. Oh, and my dad will be getting in touch with yours about the plans and the materials required."

"Is that like saying he'll be twice as busy as usual?"

"Well, maybe."

"He's really got into the idea," Annie admitted. "The work he came here for mostly just needs to be overseen. This is like a hobby for him."

"Dad said he was going to do it for free."

"I had that idea too. Mum says he earns enough from the job

he's on, so it's not like we need more money coming in."

By the time she had ended the conversation, Annie felt relaxed enough to sleep.

Wanda realised that she had dozed off again, for a quick check of her watch told her it was almost six o'clock. The slight sound of the door being opened and someone being directed in, made her instantly alert.

Thea seemed dazed, for she stopped and stared at the back wall of the room. Seeing the movement as Wanda stood up, woke her from it.

"Oh, you're here," she said, sounding relieved.

"And you look like you should sit down," Wanda told her. Thea was pale faced, but she acted on the suggestion and went to the second of the room's beds. "Isn't as bad here as I thought it might be," Wanda continued.

"I just don't know how they can think we did anything to Abbie," Thea blurted.

"I guess it is because you and your brother have a thing against her old man, and Robbo had to ring him and gloat. I assume you got the nth degree too? I had a few other questions they wanted answers to. Like why I was there and helped Abbie get there. It didn't help me that I could identify the guy who took Abbie and injured your brother."

"Who?" Thea asked.

"Better I don't say. If you don't know, you won't let it slip. Because if you did, it might make you seem more involved."

"Oh. They asked me if we had sent a ransom note. I said, 'of course not' but I don't think they believed me."

Thea didn't seem to want to volunteer anything more, so Wanda waited a while before asking, "Did they mention anything about bail?"

"No. Just something about having to appear before a judge, either tonight or tomorrow."

Wanda knew from what David had told her, that there was to

be a special sitting for them that evening.

"How is your arm," Wanda tried.

"It's okay. They gave me something that made me dopey, and used a local when they put in the stitches. I was allowed to rest for a while before they wanted me for questions. I asked about Robbo. He's still pretty bad, but they say he should be okay. He had to have surgery, and he's in Intensive care at the moment. I don't know what would have happened if you hadn't been there. Oh, you were hurt too..."

"I'm fine. I didn't need stitches, just a dressing. And I have to rest the arm." Wanda belittled her injury, and gave a snort. "At least in here, I should manage that!"

"Yeah, but we didn't do anything!"

"No, but have you considered that if they get a further call, or letter, about the ransom, they know we are here and it can't have come from us. Besides, you will probably sleep better here than at the house."

The supplied basic meal arrived then, and Wanda discontinued her attempts to get information from Thea until they finished. Even then, she had little luck, as Thea was reluctant to say anything about their disagreement with Carson without her brother around. All she said was that her brother had all the details.

Wanda decided to try again in the morning. They were both tired, and likely to fall asleep as soon as the hearing was over. Then there was no rush. Thea probably had no one to go bail for her, and in her own case bail would be allowed so that she could be pulled out when David's plan allowed.

That thought reminded her that she'd not heard anything from David through the ear receiver. There probably hadn't been a need since her task was to get Thea to talk. She hadn't asked him if the device also picked up sound around her. That was proof that she wasn't back on top of her game. Still, David probably had a plan to find out when she had all that Thea would tell her. He'd have her pulled out for more questions or something. Yes, she'd leave more probing until tomorrow.

Wanda had barely finished her breakfast when she was called out of the room. She gave Thea a 'see you later' wave and followed the uniformed officer. She assumed, that David wanted to see her, and he would be waiting for her, but the person who greeted her, and told her she was being released, her bail paid, was no one she knew. The little shiver that was the start of her 'danger sense' put her onto high alert. She tried to get an impression of what was going on, but the man seemed to be a bail agent, doing his job as usual.

"Who put up bail?" she asked, using her delinquent persona. "I thought I was going to be stuck there for ever."

The name he gave her meant absolutely nothing, and that made her even more wary. Something was afoot, but she had no reason to refuse to leave the centre, and in her persona of a fringe criminal, she wouldn't want to stay and would be glad to be out. She sent a surge of mental alarm, directed at David and hoped he wasn't asleep. If he felt that, he would check on her. Still, she delayed as much as she dared, with the formalities, before going out with the man.

"Do I get to meet my benefactor?" she asked. "He must want something from me."

"Yes. I am to take you to him," the agent said. Now she had the idea that this was not a normal part of his job, but that he'd been paid to do it. She had no proof at all if her idea was true, but she trusted these moments of 'just knowing'. In any case, this was definitely not a part of David's plan.

She was led to a black car with darkened windows, and a door opened for her. The bail agent nodded for her to get in, but he remained outside. Her danger sense was telling her this was not a good idea, but it wasn't screaming at her to run. She ducked down to get into the back seat, and as she did, she had a look at the man behind the wheel of the car.

At first she thought it was Delaney, but her nose told her otherwise. This man smelt of decay and rot, not stale sweat. He was gangly too, not solid. What had been the same was the reddish scar on his face, that was real, and not created like Mickey had done with face paint. When she moved in further and settled herself, she had a glimpse of one hand on the wheel. It had an intricate black spider tattooed on it.

"Hurry up and sit, Bitch. And you stay put and don't try to get out. I have'ta take you to the guy what paid to get you out. If you do what I say, then you might not get hurt," the man said, and he turned further and she could see his rotted teeth as he added, "I like carving flesh, you see."

Wanda had no intention of inflaming the sickness in the mind of the car's driver. He didn't have a knife where she could see it, but as he drove, he was imagining what he could do to her. From the man's description, she had a very good idea that he was the man seen at the local high school, earlier in the year. The one thought to be involved with drugs. It gave her a way to get his mind on a different track.

"You don't have any uppers, do you?" Her question surprised the man. "I intend to nick off, later, and I am going to need something so I can get well away."

"What makes you think I do?" He laughed, sounding like a sick crow.

"Just wondered. Hoped."

"Got a few," the man said, and then listed the street names of half a dozen kinds. Most were unfamiliar to Wanda.

"Great! Any chance I can stop at a bank?" Wanda put a whine in her voice, to add, "You won't give out any if I can't pay, right?"

"Yeah. Right. We'll see. You gotta go see the guy that got you out first."

"And who's that?"

"Not'ta say. He don't want you scared off, see?"

"Huh! If it's Mickey D, he'd better be scared himself," Wanda predicted.

"What did ya do'ta him, bitch?"

"Trounced him. Do it again too given half a chance."

"Don't try nothin' in here, savvy?"

"You don't give me a reason, then," Wanda countered. "Way I figure it, you'n'me don't want to stay together longer than need be, huh?"

"S'right!"

"Okay then."

The man drove away from the custody centre and seemed to grow less nervy the further away he got. Wanda didn't ask where they were going, she knew right away they were going east, and the GPS on the car's dash showed the route. She soon had the idea they were heading back towards the area she knew. She was not surprised to find she was right, but she was surprised by the destination. The man drove past Carson's house, and took the next side street, and the next again. He parked in the street parallel to Carson's street, and by her estimate, in front of the house behind his.

The driver checked the time. "Gotta wait till eleven, then you gotta meet the guy out the back, see?"

"Okay. You got time to go by a bank?"

"Later. Once you done what you gotta do."

According to the cars, dash clock, they had fifteen minutes to wait. Wanda made no secret of twisting around to check out the cars parked nearby in the street. There had been a car she was sure was a police stakeout in Carson's street.

"What ya doin', bitch."

Wanda told him. "Obviously, I am here to use my illegal skills. I am just checking for potential heat."

Just the idea of official watchers, made the man nervous. She wasn't going to tell him there were some in the other street.

"Get out. We're goin' in."

They went up the driveway of the house that was advertised for rent. Anyone seeing them would not think them suitable tenants. Wanda was told to jump a gate to get to the back yard, and that usually easy action was harder when she needed to be careful of her arm. The man followed, more agilely than Wanda had expected.

"Down the back, in that corner," Wanda was told. The man pointed, and Wanda realised it was because Carson's back yard and this one only overlapped along a short section.

The man with the tattoo told her to go over first, and Wanda knew there was someone waiting there, but the guy with her now had his knife out.

Delaney grabbed her as she turned around to survey the yard. "Got you, bitch," Delaney snarled. "I gotta job for you, and you'll do it or I gut you."

"In your dreams!" Wanda said. "You haven't the balls for it." She felt the grip on her arm tighten. It was her injured arm, and he knew it. "Only reason you're not writhing already, is that I'm happy to irritate dear Carson, a little bit more. Is this still to do with what my uncles want?"

The grip on her arm got even tighter as Delaney realised that she was related to his other problem.

"Nah, bitch. I got that so safe they'll never find it."

Wanda risked a low chuckle. It made Delaney stop and yank her around. "What's so funny?"

"I don't like them either, so I don't mind if they don't get what they want. It's nothing to me."

At that moment, from his lack of questions, she was sure Delaney knew nothing of her association with the task force that had captured him. Delaney checked his watch.

"Come on. We have twenty minutes." He began to drag her towards the back of the house. He went directly to the back door as if oblivious to the possibility of cameras as part of the security system. Inwardly she shrugged, but then he had her escort watch her while he went to work on the lock.

"Doesn't he have an alarm system?" she asked in a low voice.

"Nah! I told him to leave it off."

Wanda filed that detail away for reference, and indeed, when he dragged her inside, her danger sense didn't get any stronger. At least it didn't until they were in Carson's office.

There was enough light coming in through the open curtains to have a look around the room and compare what she saw with what had been there last time. Nothing obvious caught her attention, until she removed the picture from in front of the safe. She was just about to lean it against the wall when she spotted a trace of plaster dust on the floor. Her danger sense peaked, as she ran her hand around the bottom and sides of the safe. She felt a tingle, telling her that there was now an active alarm on the safe. She didn't mention it to Delaney, he'd never believe her, and with two knife wielding lunatics so close, it wasn't time to annoy them. Besides, she wanted them all to be caught once Delaney had the money he obviously expected to find here.

"You remember the numbers?" Delaney hissed.

"Yes," Wanda said, already trying them. She was not surprised when they didn't work. In fact it amused her. If the safe had a silent back to base alarm, was Carson hoping Delaney would be caught?

"What's wrong?"

"He's had the combination changed. Shhh! I need quiet."

Delaney hissed for his mate to go lookout, as Wanda had her right ear near the dial. She was proceeding as slow as she dared, and hiding her amusement.

She had just opened the safe when her earlier escort hissed, "Cops out front."

Delaney shoved her aside, and reached for the wrapped bundle in the safe. Wanda was already moving back towards the office door. Delaney's mate shoved her out of his way and moments later, Delaney pushed her so hard she fell against the wall. She recovered quickly, having every intention of stopping Delaney getting away, but discovered she didn't need to.

Leo Tatarovich, looked up from Delaney's unconscious form and smirked. "He's all yours. We have what we want." Without a further word, he disappeared into the shadows of the trees that bordered the yard.

"You'd better go home fast then," she said after him, as a second figure, dumped Delaney's mate beside him. "Interpol knows you are here and have agents arriving today."

Stephan gave her a wave of thanks and followed his brother.

The police challenge came mere moments later, but she didn't move or disobey the command to 'freeze'. She just moved both hands into sight to show she wasn't armed.

The first officer to reach her checked her for weapons.

Wanda surprised him by stating, "Can you please mention what you found here, on a private channel, to Superintendent Des Kingley. If he isn't already aware? The man on the ground there is Mickey Delaney. His mate, I think, is a man seen hanging around Bellfield School, earlier this year."

While the officer watched her, his partner handcuffed the two men. "And you are?" he asked suspiciously.

"Wanda Davis, attached to the Atlas Task Force. I was undercover in the custody centre to talk to a suspect when these two arranged for me to be bailed out. You will find Carson's safe is open. Delaney took that package from it, and tried to run. He needed me to open the safe. I just didn't tell him of the new alarm put on the safe. Oh, and when he broke in via the back door, he said, "Carson was told to leave the other alarms off.""

Wanda felt her hands being forced behind her, and handcuffs going on, but this time, she wasn't worried.

"Did you overcome these two?" Wanda was asked.

"Don't you think I could?" she asked, so as not to tell an outright lie. "Ask Commander Britten, he'll tell you."

It was an evasion. She didn't want to mention her uncles, but she needed to tell her boss about them as soon as possible. As she stood, calmly, the other officer went inside to use Carson's house phone. A short while later, the mobile carried by her guard, rang. By the tensing of his posture, she guessed his superior was giving him orders. The final, "Yes, Sir!" was most definite.

"How did you get here?" Wanda was asked.

"Over the back fence from the street parallel to this. That guy," and Wanda pointed because she didn't know the man's name, "drove me from town in a dark sedan with tinted windows. He may have drugs in there."

"What about Delaney?"

"I don't know. He was already in the back yard when I jumped the back fence. Both of them threatened to slice me if I didn't do as told. I didn't think I could get both of them at once, so I decided I had better obey."

"And later?"

"Their attention had wandered. They knew you had arrived and just wanted to get away."

"I have orders to have those two brought in without the gawkers outside seeing them. You, however, I can bring out openly."

"I don't suppose you are allowed to tell me why?" Wanda asked, though it was probably part of her husband's plan.

"No, but I was told you would probably figure it out."

Wanda sighed dramatically. "I am probably meant to be misdirection. Delaney told me he only had twenty minutes to be in and out. I don't know why."

"Carson is out doing a ransom drop. You know his daughter is missing, don't you?"

Wanda nodded.

"That's why we were down the street, watching. One of the higher ups expected something shady, it seems."

The officer was staring at her.

"Hey! I didn't ask to come here." She got a grim smile for that, but they were still treating her as a suspect.

She had to wait until a plain white van arrived to pick up the other prisoners who were beginning to stir.

It gave her time to think and she suddenly wondered where Carson's wife and housekeeper were. Had Carson told them to go out while Delaney was expected? Or was his wife somewhere near where the drop was to be? She asked the officer that was holding her that question. He was concerned enough to check the house before they left.

"They must be out," he told her. Wanda wondered if he was thinking that odd or convenient. In her opinion, Carson wouldn't want anyone to know he was expecting Delaney at his house.

"Thanks. I didn't like the thought that Delaney might have hurt them."

While Delaney and the other man were being loaded into the white van, she was walked out to a marked divisional wagon under the scrutiny of over a dozen gawkers. She guessed that one or more would tell Carson about her, and that he would be even more worried after that. They wouldn't see the police carrying the package of money, and he would assume Delaney had it. Only would Delaney say where he had stashed Abbie? Wanda hoped she'd be found.

Wanda was relieved when she was taken to the local police station, unlike Delaney who was headed for more secure quarters. She hoped to pick up some hint of the current state of affairs, but the station seemed deserted except for the desk sergeant, who processed her and led her to the cells.

She didn't bother to ask, "Do I have to be locked up?" These officers did not know her, and only know they had found her on private property where a robbery had occurred. The person who had given them the orders, may have been told to have her locked up to force her to rest. She was supposed to be taking it easy, and jumping fences and having your wounded arm tortured by a sadistic brute was hardly that. Besides, she had implied to the arresting officers that she had overcome Delaney and the other guy. Another activity that David would have words to her about. If her uncle hadn't been fortuitously around, she'd have done her darnedest to stop him anyway.

At least she had been allowed to have a dose of painkillers – not that they would do much. At most the over the counter drugs she could tolerate would only take the edge of the pain away. Anything stronger was likely to cause a repeat of her missing Thursday.

So Wanda decided to act docile, and use the quiet to try some mind tricks to ease the pain. Except that when considering her uncles, she wondered why they had turned up then. Had they been following and watching Delaney? Leo had said they had what they wanted, ie the envelope with the prototype's specs, so he either got the location out of Kemple, or Delaney had gone to check for himself that the specs were where Kemple put them. If she were them, she'd have taken off as soon as she had the envelope, and not worried about delivering Delaney. Maybe a promise made to another family member was sacred, so they had made sure she had the bastard. Or maybe, Leo wanted to gloat that he had the specs that the Task Force were trying to find. She finally decided the latter idea was more likely correct, but the joke was on him. And she'd had the last word. Stephan at least had appreciated the warning.

And that was not going to go down well with her boss, or the Interpol agents. Well, they might have decided to flee before now anyway. She decided there was little harm done.

One thing, she urgently wanted to know if Abbie Carson had been found, and to tell Commander Britten that The Family had found and taken the envelope they had wanted. However, as time passed, and no one came for her, she came to the conclusion that a lot was going on, and she wished intensely that she knew what.

Martin wasn't sure if he had passed out or not, but the van didn't seem to have travelled very far when he was jerked by the van stopping. He heard a racket, like a garage door opening and the van moved again. The noise resumed and when it stopped, the back door of the van was opened. Delaney shoved him out, and laughed when he fell onto a concrete floor. Before he could try to get himself up, Delaney hauled him to his feet.

He wished he could ask why he had been taken, but his attempts to speak around the tape on his mouth, were ignored as Delaney pushed him along.

"You gotta job to do for me, Boy, since your old man slunk off on me." Delaney's voice was vicious. "A kind of boy scout job, since you wanta be pally with the cops."

Martin could only wince as his shoulder hit a door frame, and again as he was pushed onto a hard chair.

"It's like this, see. The cops are expecting to see someone come out to pick up the ransom for Carson's little bitch. I am sure that lot of dough will be tagged and tracked. But I have a better plan, see. And you are gonna follow it exactly. That's if you want little Abbie to get back to her doting daddy without being changed forever. Like I mean being made like the stupid woman Carson shagged to have her."

Delaney gave no warning before ripping the tape off Martin's mouth. "Now I don't trust you worth shit, boy, so I got some incentives. You tell the police anything, and I mean anything, and I will send an anonymous tip to the drug squad about you, and what you are up to in your garage now that no one is watching you. They will find a nice little stash, too big to talk your way out of."

"You bastard!"

"All you have to do, is what I tell you, exactly. I will be having you watched all the way. I will know where you are and where the cops are all the time. Any deviation from my directions, will make me send another message to the guy you tried to dob on at your school."

Delaney gave that a moment to sink in before adding, "Your new girlfriend is a pretty thing, isn't she? Well, I know where she lives, because we followed her home."

Martin's gut twisted and he felt like he needed a toilet. He didn't want anything the happen to Abbie, or Annie.

"So that's it, boy. You in?"

"What choice do I have? Nor any guarantee you won't do as you say, anyway."

"If I get my money, you don't need to worry. I'll be away as fast as I can."

"Where's Abbie?"

"Oh, no, boy. Carson will find out when I have my money."

"What do I have to do?"

Delaney had an evil grin on his face as he swiped the blindfold off Martin's eyes and saw them to be red and watery. "Now I know you won't talk, boy. You don't need that, huh?"

Martin growled, a curse.

"What you need to know, I'll tell you tomorrow, boy. Now, I got things to check, and you and my mate here are going to stay put."

Delaney turned and walked from the room. His phone began to hum, and he answered it tersely. "Where are you, you little shit? Did you check the merchandise? What do you mean? Being followed? Since when? If you've queered the deal, it'll be the last thing you do." He was getting further away, and Martin couldn't hear any more. He turned his attention to studying the tall man still watching him.

"I need the toilet," Martin told him. "The company here gives me the shits."

"Shut up. It's through that door. No funny stuff."

"Can I have my hands free? I can't go anywhere, that bastard," Martin shrugged in the direction Delaney had gone, "will have made sure of that."

Crane considered the question for a while and then reached into his pocket for a folding knife and slashed the tape. When Martin headed in the indicated direction, Crane followed. He had swapped the knife for a gun. In the small amenities area, Crane said, "Use that one! Leave the door open."

"You some kind of pervert are you?"

Crane lashed out with a fist. "Enough of that."

The cubicle had no window, so Martin wasn't able to look out to try to figure out where he was. He could hear trucks going along the road outside, but that was little help. At least one source of discomfort was reduced before he emerged. He would try to look around. This guy wasn't as smart as Delaney, and he might give something away.

The room where he'd been taken was some kind of lunch room. It had a table and several of the hard chairs, and along one wall was a bench with a microwave and a toaster oven. Martin wondered if there was anything in the bar fridge, that was edible. He decided to go and look, and his guard didn't seem to be worried. It was empty, and turned off. One of the cupboards under the bench had mugs, so he helped himself to one and had a drink of water from the tap, and then used some water to rinse his chemical affected eyes.

The window in this room was of opaque glass, so that too gave no clue to the outside. Martin wanted to pace, but he'd only circled the room twice when his guard said, "Sit down."

"I'm bored!"

The man considered again and stood up from a chair by the table and reached into another cupboard. This time he came out with a portable radio, and turned it on. "Shut up and listen to that."

He returned to the table, and went back to circling things in a newspaper.

Martin walked past, and saw it was one focussed on horse racing. "You do any good at that?"

"I does okay."

"Reckon you can teach me?"

"Why?"

"So I have something to keep my mind from trying to get loose from here."

"Maybe. This be some system Mickey told me of."

"Anyone one ever told the horses they got to run to a system?"

"Funny guy! No, it's all based on recent performance, and who's riding and stuff like that."

"Okay. Are these races on today?"

"Yeah. We can listen on the radio."

"You putting money on?"

"Might."

Once Martin got the guy talking, and sounding superior because he knew all the stuff, he was happy to keep talking. Martin listened, and wished he had a way to write the info down. It was interesting, and did sound feasible, what with the part about considering the expert's predictions. They were the ones who had ears in all the racing stables, so they learnt the condition of each horse. But the stats for each horse were given in the paper – so you could compare the performance of each horse against the other runners.

When the first race was due to be run, the guy changed the radio station and egged on his selection by muttering the horses name. He had used his phone to make his bet, and when that one won, he smirked at his student.

The activity passed he time, until Delaney returned several hours later, with several pizza boxes. That surprised Martin, but he wasn't going to turn down food. Delaney passed one to the tall guy, he called Crane, and the next one to Martin, and kept the third.

"I got all the same. Hope you aren't some faddy eater. I like the lot on my pizza."

Delaney seemed pleased about something, and Martin didn't dare ask what. In between races and watching Crane pick his selections, he'd been trying to think why Delaney stupid enough to abduct Carson's daughter, and how he had known where she was. Why he wanted a proxy to collect the ransom was obvious. The police were after him for being got out of remand for murder. But if this was the usual type of abduction, the kidnapper usually stressed 'no police'. Or was Delaney assuming the police would ignore that anyway?

Martin took his box to the table and sat on a chair. Delaney snickered at his table manners. His comments were ignored, as Martin bit into the pizza. It was really good. He was over half way through it when he tasted something acrid, he stood and ran for the small sink and spat out the mouthful he what he was eating. Then he washed his mouth out with water.

"You got no stomach for jalapeno's boy?" Delaney taunted him.

He'd never tried whatever they were, so he assumed that was what he had eaten. However, before he'd finished another piece, he felt himself becoming sleepy, and decided to close the box and push it away.

It was all he managed to do.

Martin woke, lying on the floor, being nudged in the side by Delaney's booted foot.

"Wake up, boy. You got work to do."

"Yeah, keep your shirt on. I've got things to do first."

The way he felt, was from more than just sleeping on a concrete floor. When he stood up, and saw the pizza box on the table, he realised that Delaney must have drugged him. He swore under his breath as he made his way to the toilet, and tried to wake up by splashing cold water on his face. He might have been tempted to want to eat the rest of the pizza for breakfast, except Delaney probably wouldn't let him. If he was wanted to do decoy for Delaney, he'd have to be awake. He was somewhat more alert when he returned.

There was a hand drawn sketch on the table, and Delaney was talking in a low voice to Crane. When he heard Martin return, he broke off and gestured, "Sit there. Shut up and listen."

Using the map as an aid, Delaney detailed his plan to get the ransom. Martin listened, and all the places and ways the plan could go wrong came to mind. He was a decoy, nothing more, and he soon began to realise that Delaney wasn't counting on this succeeding. He had to have something else in mind. However, even if that was true, it didn't mean that his decoy wasn't going to be watched. The news he'd heard yesterday had said at least four men had been involved in the abduction, so there were at least two more men he hadn't seen. How could he warn the police, and warn Annie? Delaney had his phone somewhere, either on him or in the van. Maybe, if they went in that he could check?

The moment of hope was dashed, for once he could repeat the plan without mistake, Crane grabbed his arm and said, "Come on. We need to be in place early."

They didn't go to the van, but to a normal sized door next to the roll up one.

Martin had his first look at where he was. There was a park opposite, but he knew it wasn't River Park. He knew that area too well. This one may have been further along the river, and it had sections thick with trees, and open areas.

He glanced both ways along the street and only saw a row of factory or small manufacturing premises.

The one they'd been in, just one of similar ones all along the street. Crane hustled him to the end of the street.

The instructions to Carson were for him to put the case of money inside the picnic area rotunda, next to one of the barbecues, and then leave and return to his car. A message would be left as to where to find Abbie. He hadn't been given a message to leave there, so he assumed Delaney would call or something.

Crane was looking everywhere, and anyone seeing him would assume he was doing something furtive.

If Delaney was to be believed, he had instructed Carson not to tell the police about the drop, because if there were police in the park, the drop and return of Abbie would be off. However, the way he'd been talking earlier suggested that he was expecting the police to be everywhere. Martin had decided he couldn't trust anything Delaney said. Particularly after the nasty chuckle when he'd said, "No one would suspect you, boy. Chummy as you are with all the local cops."

They were early. The drop time was still three quarters of an hour away. Crane just said, it was so they'd be there before Carson, and could look see for him double crossing and having cops there. So far, Martin assumed, Crane had not seen anything to spook him. They went through the park, and approached the barbecue area from the riverside. At the edge of a thicket of trees, they stopped, out of sight, to wait for Carson. Crane hissed a warning, "You bring the case to the trees near the public toilets. Don't be seen. I'll take the money from there. You go back to the street with the case and there'll be a car waiting to pick you up. But if you see police, you run like hell, take the case, and remember if you say anything to them, your little girl friend will be scarred for life." Crane was screwing something onto the end of a gun as he spoke. That was another kind of warning. Who might he have orders to shoot? The police, or the unwilling go-between?

If this had been River Park, and the only police likely to be involved were those stationed at Kew or Bellfield, he'd have a chance to recognise them, even if out of uniform. Then he'd feel happier about being able to elude them. Instead, he felt like a duck in one of the carnival type shooting games. Delaney hadn't fooled him. If the police saw him taking the case of money, they would assume he was involved, and he'd bet anything that was what Delaney hoped.

Maybe though, they would be just as sure that he wasn't working alone, and they would leave him be in the hope he would lead them to the others. He could live with that idea, but if they only followed him, and didn't see Crane, maybe that wouldn't help. Crane must have had instructions to go in a different direction after the case swap.

Once Carson had finished looking around, as if for a note to say where Abbie was, and headed back the way he had come, Martin was told to wait a bit. He wondered why until he saw two apparent drunks teetering along the meandering footpath. They stopped near the rotunda, and began an argument, once the blows began connecting, Crane shoved him. "Now, get going."

Martin saw the opportunity to sneak around and approach from the rear. He did so, and kept low once he had the case, diving back into the cover of the trees, and heading for the toilet hut. Crane was there, and had a backpack open. He took a few moments to empty the money from the case. Martin closed it and began heading for the road. At least it was lighter if he had to run.

Resisting the urge to look around, and seem suspicious, or rather more suspicious, Martin headed for the road. He saw no car that was waiting for him, and that gave him shivers. He wasn't just going to stand there, he would head back towards the building where he'd been a virtual prisoner. He caught sight of Crane, up ahead, going in the same direction. Then he saw other people moving in on the building, and realised the police had been watching and somehow knew the money had changed hands. He glanced around, saw a car coming up behind him, and his nerve broke. He dropped the case and ran, back into the park, and zigzagging through the trees.

Episode 19

Martin's Troubles

Chapter 1

Only because Delaney had been involved in the kidnapping and was wanted by the Task Force, were David and Kelso allowed in on the action. Kelso was dressed casually, almost slovenly for him, and David was an unknown as far as Delaney was concerned, and they had organised the use of a small camera drone to observe the ransom drop site from above. David was wearing VR goggles, to steer the drone in a holding pattern above the park, high enough to be unnoticed. Kelso was with him as an observer and to relay what David saw to the police controller. They were on the roof of one of the businesses flanking the park.

The police were keeping out of the park, but in position to watch all the people going in and out. A cordon of unmarked police cars and private police vehicles were a block away on all sides. They had even allowed for the possibility of an approach by boat up the river.

After giving the area a careful scrutiny, David followed Carson from his car to the drop point, watching for followers. Carson placed the case as directed, looked around and the returned to his car, to wait.

David kept watch on the barbecue rotunda, as it was his job to watch the case closely. It did have a tracker tag inside, but it was passive. It would send no signal unless answering one directed at it. Others would be watching Carson, in his car, just as they had when he was away from it.

Ostensibly, Carson was working with the police, but he was not aware of all the actions the police were taking. If the observations proved him innocent, and word was received as to where Abbie was, Carson would be none the wiser for the suspicion. Superintendent Des Kingley had insisted on that.

"Hey! That's Martin Kemple! What's he doing here?" David exclaimed to Kelso.

"Delaney knows him," Kelso reminded him. "We know he was taken from his place, this must be why. Just let this play out. We want Delaney. He has to be around here somewhere. Can you do a quick turnaround to look where he came from?"

David took the tiny drone up higher, and focused the camera on the trees. "Nothing obvious," he reported and quickly returned the camera to the barbecue area. The plain clothes police would be casually coming in from that direction.

Martin wasn't the only person in view, but he was the closest to the case of money. Two men, both teetering as if drunk, were following the path towards the rotunda. They suddenly began to fight, and David almost missed the moment when Martin ducked into the rotunda, grabbed the case and ran back to the trees. David instinctively counted seconds while he tried to find Martin again. The trees were interfering with clear sight, and when he finally saw Martin, it was walking along the street, still with the case.

He was giving Kelso a running commentary, and added his own view that the scene he now saw was odd. Martin looked to be expecting someone to be there to meet him, but no one was near. The police in the cordon had him in sight, so David made the drone turn right around.

"Shit!" he exploded aloud. "Kelso, look at that extra monitor. Do you recognise that tall thin guy with the large backpack? I'm pinging the tracker, look for the dot."

An intake of breath showed Kelso understood. "It's not with

Martin Kemple. They switched cases. Follow that man. I'll ping it again."

Then Kelso spoke into the radio. "Kelso to all units. The money is with…" he gave the description of the man and where he seemed to be heading. A second voice gave directions to pick Martin up, discretely.

"He's going into a building. It has Harry's towing on the façade, and a large roller door," David reported calmly, even though he had heard that Martin had dropped the case and had taken off.

The police were moving in around the building, but were still keeping out of sight. They had not seen Mickey Delaney. They needed to be sure he was within the building.

Then Kelso's phone began vibrating. David couldn't see his expression, as he still had the VR goggles on, but his tone was vibrant when he said, "Excellent."

Moments later, the order was given to move in on the building. David kept watching, and from his high viewpoint, saw the tall man run out onto the sloped roof and curl himself up behind an aircon unit. Having that knowledge, the police followed, moving carefully, and the man was caught.

"Okay, wrap it up, David," Kelso directed. "They have the case, and the money."

"What about Martin?"

"They haven't got him yet. He probably knows this area better than most people. We will catch up to him."

David removed the goggles, thinking that Kelso's 'we' was probably a reflexive term meaning the police.

"What was excellent," he asked as he began to pack everything into the carry case.

"Delaney is in custody, and so is a nasty customer Stephen 'Spider' Piretti." Kelso sounded smug. "Thanks, it seems, to your wife."

"Where were they?"

"Carson's house. Someone set off the new safe to base alarm. Wanda couldn't have known of that."

"Don't you believe it! If it went off, she meant it to," David countered. "What else?"

"When the police watching the front of Carson's place arrived, both Delany and Piletti were out cold. I assume, as your wife was just waiting for them, that she took them out."

David swore. "What part of 'don't use that damn arm' doesn't she get? So who knows what right now? Was Wanda seen being taken away from there?"

"Yes, just as planned. She will be awaiting us in the holding cells at Kew. The other two were taken off later in a plain white van, which people can assume were the forensic crew. They've gone to the secure holding cells at headquarters. Commander Britten is going to be there, and intends to take on the questioning of Delaney."

"Well, that will make Wanda happier," David opined. "He can wear out his bombastic questioning technique on someone more deserving of it."

"And not on one of his Mavericks?" Kelso suggested, and David gave a quick grin. Then he took a deep breath and turned serious. "Okay. How is Abbie?"

"I haven't heard. She was going to be examined by a police doctor, and allowed to rest yesterday. I don't know if anyone has been there to take her statement, but I will find out."

"Yes. I would like to hear what she says before her father gags her," David admitted. "When will Carson be told?"

"It will need to be soon. However, we can keep it quiet a bit longer, unless Delaney left a message as to where he stashed the girl. We can say Delaney wasn't seen here, but we had some luck later and he was spotted."

"So is Des willing to wait and see if another call does come in?"

"To a point. However, we now have everyone who could be blamed for the abduction, each unaware that the others have been caught. Delaney had 25K on him, taken from Carson's safe. I had word passed to me that Carson had been told to leave the alarm system off."

"Do you think that Delaney expected to get that other 25K as well?"

"He damn well nearly did," Kelso swore. "I am assuming he did expect to get back there, to meet that tall guy, after the initial heat died down."

"So, as things seem to be, Carson will be waiting word from Mickey as to where his daughter is," David summarised.

"We will have to see if there was anything left at the drop," Kelso warned. "They will be doing a search in the area. However, Des is fairly certain that Carson doesn't know where Mickey put his daughter."

With everything packed, David followed Kelso back down to their car. David spared a thought for Martin.

"I hope Martin doesn't do anything stupid."

"I think Delaney put the fear of devil into him," Kelso suggested.

"Must have. He's a good kid who doesn't deserve that reputation he has."

"I know lad, and so do the local police. I think if all the evidence is looked at − it will be obvious he wasn't in on the actual snatch, even if Abbie was in his garage. In fact, suspicion is being cast in so many directions, that the real perpetrators have probably betrayed themselves."

Martin ran as fast as he could, heading blindly into laneways, cutting through to streets and finally backtracking by a different route, to get to the river. He considered swimming downstream to where he could get a bus or a tram somewhere. He was so totally sure that Delaney would do as he said, if he talked to the police. Surely though, now the guy had his money, Delaney would head away from Melbourne? How could he be sure though?

Finally, he had to stop, out of breath, and he berated himself for cowardice. What he needed to do was warn Annie, but he didn't want to frighten her. In any case, he needed money for the phone. His own phone was who knew where. It might even be in Delaney's pocket, along with the small amount of change he'd had. Then he remembered something his mother had once told him, before she had walked out on him. It was something about calling the operator and asking to have the charges reversed so the person he called would pay them. Could people still do that? Could you do it to a mobile? He didn't know. Just as he had no idea where there might be a public phone. These days most people had mobiles.

Finally he had the idea of seeing if a petrol station had one. He recalled his father using one there, when he still thought his father worth knowing. Before he discovered what a spineless worm he really was. He headed back to the main road and began to walk.

The cars passing him were just blurs, as he tried to figure out what to do, and who might help him. If he could call David or Wanda, he would trust their advice. But he couldn't.

The car pulling in sharply just ahead, startled him. Seeing the two men jump out and run at him, gave him new life. He tried to run, but he was almost spent. In moments, he was being held against a wall and searched. He felt the blood drain from his face when they pulled something from his pocket.

They had known to look for it, Martin realised. He hadn't put it there. In fact he had believed his pockets were empty. They were speaking to him, but the blood pounding in his ears deafened him and he wanted to be sick. Mickey knew he had run, He had done as he threatened.

Finally the question penetrated. "Where did you get this?"

They didn't like, "I don't know. It isn't mine." Nor did they take kindly to his question, "Who are you?"

One of them did draw out his ID and confirm his worst fear. "Garret, Drug Squad."

He was handcuffed and bustled into the car. He felt he had just stepped onto the road to hell.

At the police station, the one he knew from recent events, he caught sight of DC Kelly who glanced over, but said nothing. Even his expression, neutral though it was, felt censorious. He was bustled through to the cells, none to gently, shoved into one, and then had the door locked behind him. He stumbled forward, turning to curl up on the floor between the bed and the washbasin. Tears were flowing freely, and he couldn't stop them. He was totally unaware of anything outside of himself until a nearly tuneless humming stopped the fears swirling madly in his head.

He looked up, moved his head and met the concerned gaze of Wanda.

"What....What are you doing in there?"

"Waiting to be debriefed," she said, just loud enough for him to hear.

"Don't you mean questioned?"

"Pedantics!" Wanda dismissed the question. "What about you?"

Martin felt his throat close up. He really, really, wanted to tell her. But she was like the police. Would have to tell them what he said. Mickey said he'd know...

"Shit!" Wanda exclaimed aloud, startling him out of his fears again. "I'm not meant to be saying anything about this, Martin, but if it is Mickey that you are scared shitless about, he can't hurt you now."

"He'll go after Annie, or get one of his mates..."

"God. I hate that man," Wanda exploded. She seemed to consider something for a moment. Then she said, "He can't."

"What?"

Wanda just looked at him, not saying anything more. It reminded him of how she'd let him figure out how to do what she explained about the locks.

"He can't," she had said. Elation began to bloom. Did that mean they'd caught him?

He saw Wanda nodding slowly, and was reminded of how Annie had said she'd been in Maude's head. Could she know what he was thinking?

Now he saw her tap the side of her nose. She had to be able to, and somehow, that was all he needed. To know he had an ally, even though it looked like she was in trouble too. He wanted to ask, "How come?" but he was pretty certain she wouldn't say. If Delaney was caught, Annie wasn't in danger.

Wanda nodded, and then he felt the oddest sensation in his head. It wasn't from relief, for he thought he heard, "All will work out."

Martin took a deep calming breath, and then another, until his shuddering eased and stopped.

The loud, demanding tones of Jeremy Carson disturbed the silence. Martin tried to make out the words, and noticed that Wanda was equally intent. They still hadn't found Abbie and the ransom had disappeared. She could be dead! What were the police doing?

"Jerk!" Wanda said with quiet intensity. She stood and turned, as if hearing better with that ear.

Martin saw the flesh coloured bandage over her left ear and wondered what had happened.

"How come?" Martin responded to her exclamation.

Wanda glanced his way and shook her head. He figured that she couldn't tell him, and in any case, someone had convinced Carson to calm down. They both had no choice but to go back to just passing the time. Only now, Martin felt he needed to pace the small area.

After some time, footsteps approached, and Martin spun around, saw David and asked, "What's going to happen to me?"

Startled, David said, "I don't know. I just got back here."

"So, did you finally come to get little me," Wanda growled, feigning annoyance.

"Not yet. There's a couple more lions to come before they start making a meal of you. I've come to check that ear of yours."

"It hasn't fallen off yet."

"And you haven't heard anything I sent to you, have you?"

"You haven't said anything!" Wanda stared back at her husband. "OH!"

"And that's why you are here! It's the only way they know to keep you away from trouble. Now, you need to tell me if you hear anything. I am going to send tones at different frequencies."

Each time David looked up from a data pad he'd taken from a slender satchel, Wanda shook her head. He tried one last tone and finally got a nod.

"Well, seems you can hear a dog whistle." He was grinning as he said it.

"Are you calling me a bitch?"

"Wouldn't dream of it! I will tell Britten that you couldn't receive, and I will have him find a specialist to look at that ear of yours. You had best not try climbing. Your balance might be off.”

David heard her low curse as he closed up the data pad.

“Can you do something about Martin’s face?”

“Ah, no. They’ll be wanting to rub some swabs over him.”

“But I didn’t know about the stuff,” Martin protested as he came and gripped the bars.

David said nothing, just tapped up under his own chin, and headed away.

Martin’s spirits sank, until Wanda’s soft voice muttered, “We’re being kept out of trouble, and personally, I think you have less to worry about.”

Martin didn't feel quite so confident when someone came and was let into the cell with him. The drug detection equipment was familiar to him from earlier in the year when he had been brought in. The sensor wand was run over his clothes, changing its tone when they moved it around his back and the back of his pants. It also registered something on the backs of his hands. His hands were swabbed, front and back separately. The technician thanked him and was let out.

"I'm gone," Martin moaned, forgetting he had an audience.

"You don't know what gone means, you know," Wanda told him before he sank back into apathy. "Why don't you go back over everything you remember? Just in your mind, what happened today, where you sat, places you might have recognised, concentrate on the details."

It was a good idea, but Martin had a question. "Are you really in trouble?"

"You don't need to worry about me."

Kelly did the honours, bringing Wanda from her cell and allowing her to freshen up somewhat before bringing her into the only room in the station where a dozen people could sit in relative comfort. It was the open plan area where the detectives had desks.

Only the officers and detectives involved in the day's events were present, there were only two that Wanda hadn't met. Commander Britten gestured her towards a chair that made her the focus of all the eyes.

"I believe you know everyone here, except Gordon Forrest, the Assistant Chief Commissioner for Crime, and William Floyd, one of the Forces's legal officers."

Before she sat down, Wanda went to each of the two just

introduced and shook hands. Then she moved the indicated chair so that it was behind a vacant desk. She summed up the attitude of the people present in an instant, and since Commander Britten was most rigid, she didn't begin with, "Okay, what do you all want to know?" She let him stand up and bring up each subject.

The legal officer interrupted before she could begin to speak. "How much of today's events are you aware of?"

"Only what I was doing," Wanda stated. She had hints of more, now, but her statement was true. "I don't know what my partner was meant to tell me, because as far as I knew he said nothing. I surmise his little device wasn't working after all. I assume you know about that?"

Some obviously didn't but some heads were nodding.

Britten added, "I have brought everyone up to date on events prior to today. Why don't you start from this morning and telling us what you did."

Wanda nodded, "I was occupying a cell in the city, expecting Thea Mainwright to join me. I knew her to be one of two people trying to provoke Jeremy Carson. She and her brother apparently believe, that he is their father. Last night, when she came, we were both too tired to talk much. I figured I would have time in the morning."

There was more head nodding, so she knew they had heard of the plan.

"Before I could do more than commiserate at being in our shared space, the guy in charge had me taken out. I was being bailed. I knew this wasn't part of the plan, since in reality I wasn't facing real charges. However, it told me that someone was either afraid I would tell the police something, or they needed me to do something. Either way, I was ready for trouble, and not completely helpless."

"Did you find out who had paid your bail?" Kingley asked her.

"No. The agent, I am certain, was paid for his silence. He made it clear though that I wasn't free to walk off. He did say I was to go to the person who arranged bail. Even then, the first guy I met was someone I had never met, but I believe is the man described by some of the students of Bellfield College, as being on school grounds the day school went back."

"Describe him!" Kaspersky directed. Wanda did, and the description was detailed.

"Stephen 'Spider' Piretti," Kaspersky confirmed.

"That man is a psychopath," Wanda added. "In case you aren't aware, he told me he like carving human flesh. He was trying to scare me, and while I didn't dismiss the threat, it didn't work. Instead, I distracted him by asking him if he had any uppers, and implied I intended to take off and would need them. He asked why I thought he had, and I said I just hoped, but he listed a few things he might have."

Wanda repeated the list verbatim, using the local street names. "Some of those I don't know."

Kingley glanced at David, who just shook his head. He didn't know them either.

"I kept begging for him to take me to a bank, but he said he wouldn't until after I'd done what I had to do. After that we had a cautious truce, and agreed we'd like the least time possible in each other's company. I did make a guess at the identity of my patron, and the guy wondered what I had done to Mickey."

"And you were correct?" Kingley prompted.

"Well, he may not have put up the money, but he was the guy I had to meet. Piretti drove to the street behind Carson's place, after driving past the stakeout in Carson's street. I didn't mention that, the guy was nervy enough until we'd got away from the police station in town."

"Where did you park?" Kelly asked.

"I told the two guys who abducted me from there," Wanda said. "Haven't you found it?"

"No," Kelly admitted.

That reminded Wanda that her uncles had been around. Perhaps they had used it to get away? She mentally shrugged before continuing her report, telling of going through the garden of the house, jumping the fence and encountering Mickey Delaney. Then, quite emotionlessly, mentioned everything she'd done and thought and said, and the little Mickey had told her.

As expected, they wanted her to go over the details, several times, testing her recollection. David, from his position to the rear of the group, was grinning. It took some people a while to realise her phenomenal memory. His main attention was on the Assistant Chief Commissioner and the legal officer. They would be the ones to decide if she should be charged in relation to breaking into Carson's safe. He hoped they knew the reputation of Delaney and Piretti.

Finally they let her finish. At first though, she didn't mention her uncles and their help. Wanda told herself that they were peripheral and the locals didn't need to know.

"How did you overcome Mickey Delaney?" Kingsley asked.

Wanda turned slightly, "Commander Britten, how much of Task Force matters can I mention?"

"Since Delaney is a common denominator in this and other matters, and everyone here can be discreet, go ahead."

"I didn't," Wanda answered the question. "There were two other people around – not involved in what I had to do. I believe they had been following Delaney for their own purposes. Leo and Stephan Tatarovich."

"Yes, we are aware of them," the assistant commissioner confirmed. "You are related to them, I believe?"

"Yeah, unfortunately. They would have liked to have terminated Delaney, for interfering in their business, but there was still more I wanted to learn from him. The uncles and I had an informal deal. He was mine when they had finished with him.

Leo decked him, I think, and then Stephan brought up the other guy. They didn't stick around."

"So, they have taken the missing specs," Britten suggested.

Wanda said, blandly, "I am afraid so. Leo was being unbearably smug. I gather that little detail is no surprise?"

"No," Britten admitted. "The locker has been under close watch since we returned the envelope there. We didn't recognise the person who took it out. Perhaps you could help us identify him."

"Sure," Wanda agreed. She was glad that part of David's plan had also worked.

Kingley addressed her. "However it came about, we are glad to have Delaney back in custody. He will be kept in isolation for now."

The feeling in the room had become less hostile, so Wanda dared to ask, "So, can I now be told about everything else that happened today?"

Kingley glanced at his superior, and received a nod. "We had several pieces of luck," he began. "We had Abbie Carson back safe, yesterday…"

Wanda looked at David who just shrugged at her. He had probably tried to tell her at some point. Wanda listened to the distilled details, and it wasn't hard to work out what some minds were thinking. Poor Martin, he was stressing enough from the planted drugs.

"So that's why you have Martin locked up? They set him up!"

"There is more to it than that," Kingley told her.

"And he is not the only one that is being set up," Britten warned.

"Me? Yeah. I'm a regular patsy," Wanda said neutrally. "Apart from having me open a safe, under duress, I will add, and unless Carson admits it was for the second time, what have you got?"

"That you look Abbie Carson to Footscray. You were at the house when the raiders broke in, and you were taken into custody with the regular occupants of the house."

"Is that Carson's extrapolation from media speculations? I didn't hear all his tirade. So?"

The answer to that came from the AC. "Carson began by blaming the Mainwrights for organising the abduction. He has a recording of the male asking if he had lost anything."

"Robbo was stupid," Wanda agreed.

"Carson asked about you," the Assistant Commissioner spoke with mild insinuation. "The woman who had also been at the house in Footscray. He is now claiming that you arranged it, and is demanding that you be questioned, until you tell where his daughter is. What is your take on that?"

"Can I take is as said, that you all know I was taken along by my uncles when they visited him? That was the night when I, um, went off my head."

She got nods and a couple of looks of new suspicion.

"Carson cornered me when I was trying to recover my phone. So he had me connected to the uncles and their business. I don't recall what happened after that."

David spoke up. "You fell into his Jacuzzi and probably addled yourself."

That was probably true. Wanda shrugged. "Anyway, it wasn't until Abbie Carson recognised me that I was jolted back to sense. Well, I slowly got there. When Delaney and the other three kicked in the doors, I recognised him, even though he had disguised himself. He gave himself away."

"How was that?" The AC pushed.

"Earlier, the day before, I had given him a thrashing. I merely asked if he wanted another lesson. He looked to be intending to prove his dominance, but that's when we started to hear sirens."

"Would you think that Carson knew of your relationship to the two Mainwrights before then?"

"What relationship? Robbo only ever spoke to me once, and that time it was only to tell me to shove off."

"We have a recording of a taped conversation – Carson on his phone to someone. Unfortunately, we can't use it or admit to having it. It seems to relate to the unannounced visitors he had. Do you recall?"

Wanda nodded, recalled the time and place, and repeated the conversation verbatim. This was a test, because one of the local Task Force attached officers was quickly writing down what she said. She wasn't surprised when David came over and played the recording.

"Incredible," the AC admitted as he read the transcript of her recitation, as the recording was played. "It is an odd conversation, and I believe you propose he was talking to Mickey Delaney."

"He mentioned the name Mickey," Wanda reminded her audience. That tape was played again to confirm.

"Yes, it does seem that Carson and Delaney have a prior history," the AC accepted.

Kingley made a comment. "Carson hasn't mentioned the visit of the foreigners, or finding you in the house. Do you think he knows you were recording?"

"He knew. But I told him it was just while I was in his office." She told them what she had said. "He saw me open his safe, but I don't think it occurred to him that I was scouting his house with Stephan before that."

"He does know that you have encountered Delaney," the AC warned. "He could use that against you."

"But, he'd have to admit to being visited that night, and I think he's smart enough to know that would be a minefield."

"He might assume you were doing unsanctioned things," Britten proposed.

"Or they try to get you thinking that so I would be in trouble, yeah," Wanda grinned wryly. That was where she was right then.

"Well, that links Carson to knowing Delaney, and what you could do," the AC agreed. "It is still a reach to his having told Delaney to go fetch his daughter."

Wanda knew the AC would have had her statement from the previous night. "There was time. Abbie told me when she left. She had a GPS function on her phone. I bet Carson had a tracker app on his phone, linked to hers. He may well have known where the Mainwrights were staying, since he'd had papers served on them. I didn't take the card out of Abbie's phone until we were nearly at the place. Her destination would not have been a great leap of logic. He had it confirmed by Robbo's call, which can't have been before 1.30am. Carson wanted to keep Abbie within reach. He wouldn't want the Mainwrights to have a hold over him. He needed to get her back and couldn't go himself. He knew how to force Delaney to help and if I say so, his current state of anxiety is richly deserved."

She dared anyone to contradict her. "And from what you told me, he had things set up to have her put in a storage unit, hired under Robbo's name, until his minion decided to up the ante and put the screws on him."

"Very eloquent, Mrs Davis," the AC commented.

"Have you questioned Robbo and Thea yet?" Wanda asked, in a less contentious tone.

"No. The girl won't say anything, and the man is still in intensive care." The AC turned to Kelso. "So, it is also your contention that Carson is consorting with Delaney, with the aim of getting control of the Hartley fortune."

Kelso nodded.

"When do you propose to tell him the girl is safe?" the AC demanded.

Kelso didn't look as uncomfortable as Kingley did just then, but he was no longer officially on the force.

"There are still unanswered questions," Kelso pointed out. "That's why I think you need to talk to Martin Kemple, about his part in this."

"I had that intention. What do you think he could tell us?"

"I don't know, Sir," Kelso admitted. "However, we have heard that Carson agreed to give Delaney 50K. The ransom message sent to Carson only mentioned half that amount. So while we were following the drop instructions, Delaney was getting himself into Carson's safe, through doors that should have had active alarms on them, with a convenient to blame safe-cracker."

Wanda pointed out, "Carson told Delaney he only had 10K in his safe, and when my uncle took everything out, the bundle of notes looked to be that amount. He may have stashes elsewhere, to make up to 25K. The ransom would be a convenient reason to cover the amount Delaney demanded."

"Yes, that point has been made," the AC told her. "However, Carson is right. He did as directed, no message has come about Abbie. We have Delaney, so he can't send one. Carson knows his safe was raided, and we caught someone, that had no money on her. What do you think Carson is expecting as the next move?"

David spoke up again. "I would tell him that you captured the messenger from the park. That will get him thinking that Delaney got half his payment and still wants the rest."

"And as Delaney isn't actually free?" the AC prodded. "What exactly are you saying?"

"Well, you can probably think of a variety of scenarios, but a logical next development could be an irate kidnapper making threats and still wanting the rest of his payment," David explained. "If, according to our contention, Carson is involved, he will want to continue having us think he is not. When Delaney doesn't send another message, and if Carson can't reach him, he would have to do it himself."

The AC asked, "Did you trace the number the last call came from?"

"No, it is an unregistered pre-paid phone," Kingley reported. "Anyway, how could he do it himself?"

David had a ready answer. "Use an untraceable phone to dial his home number and play a recording."

There was more discussion of details, but it was the AC who had the final say. "I am satisfied that the train of evidence is solid, and that we do have an excellent time line of events and where people were. Where possible, we should get corroborating information from phone records, CCTV footage, whatever we can. Otherwise, the information will be jumbled by a good defence lawyer. However, I do not think we can justify keeping the media blackout and keeping Abbie's return secret from her parents for too much longer. Then if we are to charge Carson, you will need to bring him in."

Kingley nodded.

"You have someone with Robert Mainwright?"

"Yes, sir."

"I want a statement from him as soon as he can give us one... just on this abduction business - nothing else. From what you have told me, the other business between him and Carson is a civil matter."

"Yes, Sir."

"Commander Britten, I think you should have your team member checked over by a police surgeon." All eyes went to Wanda, who protested, "I'm okay."

"I could make it an official order," the AC said. "Or I could have you charged with illegal entry and safe breaking and taken to hospital under guard. We've all heard your admission."

"I was coerced!" Wanda retorted at once. "And I didn't break that damn safe, I have more skill than that!"

The AC smiled faintly, and said, "Either way, I am sure you won't mind some police protection."

Wanda saw her husband smirking, and merely said, "Whatever."

Having made his point, the AC rose to leave, followed by the legal officer. "We'll be off, I want to let you question the Kemple boy without all of us present, but I want a report of the interview as soon as possible."

"Will I still be needed to talk to Thea Mainwright?" Wanda asked.

"Only if Commander Britten allows you back on active status."

The room cleared, and Kingley came over to where Wanda had been leaning on the table. "You really don't look well, Mrs Davis."

"I'm fine," Wanda repeated, but she knew she was faking. "I could use something to eat and drink. I've had nothing all day."

Kelly went out and came back with water, and the promise of food, soon. He went to Kelso and spoke quietly in his ear. The latter went off with Kelly to where the rest of the Task Force waited. David looked up to see if he was wanted as well.

"Why don't you update your wife on the other matter?" Kelso suggested, and he saw Wanda's interest.

David nodded and moved a chair closer to hers. "It's fairly certain that Leo and Stephan left on a charter flight from Avalon Airport. The flight is being tracked, although it will probably drop off the radar at some point."

"I wonder if the stolen car the Spider guy was driving ended up at that airport," Wanda suggested. David shrugged. It wasn't an important detail.

"How's that arm?"

When Wanda flinched just from his light touch, he didn't let her protest. He moved the lapel of her jacket and swore. "You've been bleeding, and not just a little. So don't give me that 'I'm okay' line." He pulled out a clean handkerchief and told her, "Hold that on the wound."

"Dav, I want to be here when Martin is questioned."

"No! Kingley has a doctor coming and if he says you go to get that seen to, you will. You've done enough for now, but you still need to play the suspect a bit longer. I will tell him to put you near Robbo. We need more than just a denial to being part of the abduction from him. You will be the best one to try talking to him."

"Alright," Wanda agreed grudgingly. "Just don't be too hard on Martin."

"It's not up to me. Kaspersky has the job, and he and Kelly know him. I will still be here, so sit quietly, and drink some water to replace lost fluids."

Wanda stood and moved away from the centre of the room. She used her good arm to position a chair near to another of the desks. That act of defiance was all she could manage, and she found she needed to prop her head up on her bent arm. She didn't try to maintain the fake expression anymore. David knew her too well to be fooled.

Wanda felt Martin's fear as he was escorted into the room. He seemed to relax a bit when he recognised Kelly and Kaspersky as well as David. He even managed a faint smile when Kelly passed him a bottle of water. She didn't sense much more after that.

Martin didn't dare tell all when he was answering questions. He was glad that it was Kelly and Kaspersky he had to deal with, not the two drug squad guys. They didn't know him. It was only when they got to the question of, "Why did you run?" that he wanted to sink into the floor. They would be convinced he was lying. "I had to warn Annie." He said so quietly that he had to repeat it.

"And later?" Kaspersky persisted. "Why didn't you stop when directed? Was it because you had drugs in your possession?"

"No!" Martin almost yelled. "I didn't know the stuff was there. They took everything from my pockets, even my loose change. If they didn't put it in then, they could have done it when they knocked me out for the night." He was finding it hard not to break down.

"What about the bag you dropped before you took off?"

"Huh? It was empty. The tall guy, Crane, took all the money out."

He had an unpleasant feeling he was missing something. Kaspersky was staring at him.

Then Kaspersky put down Martin's wallet, phone, change and the other oddment's he'd had in his pockets.

"In your favour," Kaspersky allowed, "the drug swab we did on your things came back negative. And the results of those done here only showed faint traces. Where did you sit down?"

Now Martin understood Wanda's advice. He thought carefully. "In the van they had me in," he said.

"Which was stolen," Kelly told him.

"And the building. Down from the park. It had some kind of

staff kitchen with chairs, and something like an office. I woke up this morning lying on the floor there."

Kaspersky threw an unrelated question at him. "Did you go into your garage when you went home from the park on Friday?"

"No. Why would I? It only has junk in it, mostly the old bastards stuff. Anyway, Mickey grabbed me before I even got into the house."

Kaspersky waited for him to say more, sensing he was holding back.

The sense of falling into a deep hole increased. Martin knew he dared not suggest that there might be drugs in his garage.

Then a voice from somewhere nearby had him jerking around. "Tell them everything. It's okay."

"Shit! You look like a ghost!"

Martin tore his eyes from Wanda and looked at David. Wanda was white faced and looking much worse than she had in the cells.

"Oh, there's a doctor coming to look Wonder Woman over. She tore a scab off a nasty deep graze, that's all." David kept his tone light and unconcerned.

Kaspersky drew Martin's attention back to the subject. "What aren't you telling us? Right now, in addition to possession of a commercial quantity of drugs, you are in line for a charge of accessory to kidnapping. So, if you 'didn't want to do it', why did you?"

"Is Delaney back in custody?" Martin dared to ask. He saw a slight reaction as a muscle twitched in Kaspersky's cheek.

"Is he the reason you have been so impossible?"

Martin nodded miserably.

"Yes, he's in custody," Kaspersky confirmed.

Wanda added, "And so is that creepy guy you saw at school on the first day."

Martin slumped with relief, and began to talk freely, but Kaspersky's question of a while back made him stop what he was saying. "Why did you ask if I went into my garage?"

"Were you afraid we'd find something?"

Martin nodded. "Mickey said he'd planted stuff there."

"He did put something there," Kaspersky admitted, watching Martin's face lose colour.

Kelly took pity on him. "No, we found Abbie Carson in there."

Martin felt himself grow cold. "Is she okay? I mean, how did she get there? I gave you the key to the lock. You looked in there on Thursday."

"There was a different lock," Kelly told him. "And I know you don't drive, and where you were all morning prior to her discovery."

"But, how did you find her? Were they going to come back? She could've..."

David, intent on Martin's narrative, caught movement and saw Wanda trying to stand. He wasn't quick enough to catch her. He eased her into a comfortable position on the floor and checked the pad she'd been holding on her wound. "Can someone chase up that doctor?"

Kelly went out, and David said to Kaspersky, "Aren't you convinced yet?"

The senior detective grunted before admitting, "Your friend, Annie Jamieson, apparently came back to tell you something because you weren't answering your phone. She found where you dropped your food, or that dog of hers did. She reported you missing and convinced the operator to call Kelly. By the time we got there, the dog was trying to dig into the garage. We expected to find you inside, hurt or worse."

Martin gulped, and glanced to where David had put Wanda into the recovery position. He wondered if she had survived 'or worse'.

Kaspersky went on, "We also have a statement from your neighbour about a white van backing into your drive, right down to the garage. A different one to the one you described. That was at a time when we have witnesses to say that you were still at the park or getting food."

In Martin's mind was the thought, He probably thought I'd be arrested too. Then another thought occurred to him. "Was my father a part of this? Delaney told me he'd gone and wimped out on him and that was why I had to do it."

"We don't know," Kaspersky admitted. "I will get a call put out to bring him in for questioning."

"What's going to happen to me now?" Martin finally dared to ask.

Kelly answered, "We'll be keeping you here while we get your statement typed up, and you sign it. We have to send it through to Melbourne. After that, I believe the drug squad want to talk to you."

David said, "And I intend to see that you get someone to represent you, even if I have to pay that someone myself."

For some reason, Martin felt there were still unpleasant surprises awaiting him, but when he saw a suited stranger entering, he forgot his fears while worrying about Wanda. He didn't see Kelly leaving, as he was watching the doctor as he crouched beside his patient.

"You won the lottery," Kelly spoke to him unexpectedly.

"Huh?"

"I only ordered one lot of sandwiches for you, but since our friend over there isn't in any condition to eat, you might as well have both lots. Keep the water as well."

Constable Parnell came to escort him back to the cells as a pair of ambulance attendants brought a patient trolley in. "Come on, Kemple."

Martin didn't resist. He felt better for having told everything, and from hearing how Annie had helped him again, and that Abbie was safe. He felt he could eat now. Best of all, having David's absolute belief in his innocence, with his declared intent of finding him a legal rep, was like having a father who cared coming to help him. He just hoped that someone would tell Annie he was okay.

It was a lot later, when he was on the verge of sleep from boredom, that he wondered why Carson hadn't known that Abbie was found.

It was no consolation to find himself experiencing what he had wished on his father. Being locked up on suspicion of serious criminal activities, was not what he thought he'd be doing on the weekend. He hadn't actually been charged with anything when he was taken to the city and into a room for more questioning, this time by the two men who had arrested him the day before.

This time, he wasn't sure what to say, fearing these more cynical officers would twist everything he tried to say. His cousins had been questioned a time of two and they had told him this repeatedly.

All he said, was a repeat of what he had said the day before. He did not know how the packet of white powder had got into his pocket.

He hadn't answered any of the leading questions they tried to trick him with, and they finally told him, "You expect us to believe you are not involved in selling drugs? When you were brought in and questioned, late last year? And again at the start of this year? We have statements from half a dozen students naming you as their supplier."

"Then you should also have one saying it was not possible as I was elsewhere at the time," Martin said, annoyed at himself for getting angry.

"Oh, yes, your girlfriend. How did you get her to lie for you?"

"She was telling the truth! She didn't even know what I had been accused of at the time."

They had sensed his weakness, and were attacking again, when a man was escorted into the little room.

"Officers, I have been appointed to represent this young man. I would like to talk to him in private."

He produced his identification laminate, and stared at the two detectives until they retreated.

Martin breathed easier. David had come through on his promise.

"I'm Anthony Chan. As I just mentioned, I have been retained to represent you." The man sat down in the other chair, one of two vacated by the detective. "How old are you?"

"Fifteen."

"I see. I am told you are an emancipated minor."

"Yes."

"That should not be a reason to treat you like an adult offender. Now, tell me what this is about?"

Martin explained all that he could, mentioning the powder found on him the previous day and who he believed was behind it and why. Chan nodded, "Yes, I was given a copy of your statement. What about the case you dropped yesterday before you ran?"

"What about it?"

"Haven't they told you what they found in there?"

"No."

Martin paled as he listened. "How can they think I owned that? The case came from Carson, and I had no time or reason to put anything in there, and it was Crane who took all the money out."

"Exactly! I see now, why your friend asked me to help you. I think it should be easy enough to have any proposed charges dropped."

Episode 20

Finding facts

<u>Chapter 1</u>

David wanted to go with his wife to the hospital, to be certain she would be fine, but as she was playing the role of a bailed offender, it was better that he wasn't seen hovering over her. Kelso noticed his abstraction.

"David!"

Hearing his name had David looking up, almost desperate for a distraction.

"Kingley has a task for you, if you have no objection."

"What can I do?"

"We need to question Abbie Carson, and be discreet about it."

"So you want me to do that? Being really formal, or friendly?"

"However you think is best. She has been sedated much of today. I am not sure if she realises how much time has passed since we found her. We don't want to make an issue of it, but we don't want her to blurt out when she was found. The doctor has given us permission to talk to her, and she has calmed down from when she arrived there."

"When do I need to go?"

"They will let you see her if you go now. We will need a thorough debrief, getting as much detail as you can. When the statement is written up, it will be sticking to the basic facts. Now, in theory, the girl should have a parent present for questioning, but we can either have a policewoman brought in, or have a nurse present."

"A nurse would mean one less person who knows what is going on," David suggested.

"True. You asked about your approach, well, keep it business like. I think, with you not being a policeman, the girl will be more relaxed."

"Has she wanted to go home?"

"She only mentioned it once, and seemed happy when told that her parents would be allowed to visit after she had a good night's rest."

"I expect she thinks her father will come down on her like a ton weight," David guessed. "So, who will I need to ask for at the hospital?"

"Jepson. He's head of security. Meanwhile, I will be taking over the phone monitoring team at midnight. Call me when you have the report."

David went back to Kelso's house and had a quick shower and changed into fresh clothes. He usually preferred to be inconspicuous, but this time he needed to catch Abbie's interest and encourage her to talk.

He would also have to be the perfect, courteous gentleman.

While in the bedroom he and Wanda shared, he went through his small case of electronic gadgets and took out a small voice recorder, as well as a normal paper pad and pens.

At the hospital, he was escorted into the security area, and left with the nurse in charge. She explained that Abbie was the only patient in the section, but she was currently awake and not ready to settle down.

"I will require someone else to be present when I talk to Abbie, do you have the time?"

"Certainly. Her room is number three."

At the room, the nurse knocked, and poked her head in. "Abbie, you have a visitor," she said.

Abbie, who had been watching something being streamed through the room's IT terminal, looked to see who it was. "Who are you?"

David introduced himself using the alias that matched his ID. "I have come so you can tell me what you remember about what happened to you."

"Are you some kind of psychologist?"

"No, I am working with the police to find the people who abducted you."

"Then can I go home? I want to see Mum."

"She will be allowed to come in tomorrow. We are still looking for your abductors."

"Oh, okay."

"The police have a watch on the place where you were found. We are hoping that the people will go back there, not realising that we have found you."

"Kemple? He shouldn't be hard to find," Abbie said dismissively. "I recognised his place, even half zonked."

"Yes, it was his place, but he has an excellent alibi for the time when you were put there. He was with the SES helping to look for your new phone. It was pinged, and the location received told us it was somewhere in Riverpark. It was found there, as were your shoes."

Abbie scowled. The lack of shoes and outdoor clothes were the only things keeping her there. "You won't mention that phone to my dad, will you? He doesn't know I have it, and if he did, he would take it. He took all my data off me, and deleted the numbers of all my friends. When can I have it back?"

"I think it will be needed for evidence, but I can ask for you."

"Thanks," Abbie said, trying to sound less aggrieved.

"You sound like you are bored," David said, glancing around. "You've got Foxtel."

"40 channels of crap," Abbie complained. "The news channel is blocked."

"I can understand you wanting to get back to your Mum and Dad. They are doing all they can to help bring your abductors to justice."

David watched some of the belligerence abate, and stored the reaction to consider. He encouraged her to talk before introducing the need for a statement. Questioning people was something he had trained himself to do, and Abbie, young and naïve, was no challenge.

"Tell me about your Thursday," he invited. Then asked, "Do you mind if I record you. My note taking is horrible and I don't want to misrepresent you."

"Whatever," Abbie shrugged. She waited for David to set it running on her bed table and began.

"Mum and I were up with some relatives. Her nan was meant to be sick."

"Meant to be?"

"Yeah, but she seemed okay to me, just real old."

"Go on."

"We were in the middle of nowhere's ville. No damn internet, the phone signal was weak and useless," Abbie wasn't trying to hide her annoyance. "Mum said we'd be there a week or so, but out of the blue, Dad rings up and tells Mum to come back to Melbourne. By bus! Have you ever had to spend hours on a bus? I don't know why we couldn't have just flown back. It took us all day, starting before it was even light. We had to stay in town that night. Daddy had booked a suite for us."

"I expect you would have been tired," David suggested.

"Tired of being bored," Abbie agreed. "Mum wanted to get her hair done, and said I could too. Like it?"

"It suits you very well," David agreed. "Did the hotel have a decent restaurant?"

"Mum got room service, but she said it was as good as we're used to."

"What else did the suite have?"

"I could watch Netflix. It had wi-fi too, so I could get some stuff from the internet."

"So why did you decide to leave?" David put a touch of confusion in his voice.

Abbie stopped looking at him and he thought she was going to clam up. He didn't press her.

"Because it began to feel like a prison. A nice, pleasant, but I am not allowed to leave jail."

"Why was that?"

"I wanted to go home. Where all my stuff is. I couldn't take much with me. I don't know why Daddy wouldn't let us go home."

"Did you ask him when he came to see you?"

"How do you know he did?"

"He mentioned it. He said you'd been glad to see him."

"I was. I thought he would take us home, but all he wanted to do was talk to Mum."

"What about?"

"Stuff. I watched Netflix and had to put headphones on so it wasn't so noisy."

David hit a brick wall when he asked again why she decided to leave. He knew her answer, "I was going to go home," was a lie. She didn't answer the part about, "in the middle of the night."

"Wanda told me that you had directions to a place in Footscray, and she decided to tag along."

Gradually, he teased out the full story, along with what she had overheard. It seemed that Abbie had been starving for someone, uncritical, to talk to. She didn't even get angry when David suggested that what she had done had been stupid. He decided she had already admitted that to herself.

"I think your Dad wanted you to be safe," David suggested. A minor eruption ensued.

"He's one to talk! They went off on business, I tried to call them to tell them that Mrs Hansen couldn't come, but they wouldn't answer. I mean, he always says, "we're only a phone call away in an emergency.' And when I did need them, where were they?"

"Did they give you the name of the places where they were staying?"

"No. I had their mobile numbers. They didn't want me to call the hotel in case the message went astray."

"Didn't they call to check up on you?"

"Well, no! They assumed Mrs Hansen was with me."

"What about when the house was broken into?"

"Did Dad tell you that? He didn't bother reporting it. He's been really bad-tempered since then though."

"But you got onto them about that?"

"Finally! I called Mum and I think she had to go and tell Dad. She rang back and called me on a different phone."

"How did you know that?"

"Duh! I have Mum's and Dad's programmed. This wasn't one

I knew.”

“Of course!” David pretended to be sheepish.

David wanted to bring Robbo and Thea back up, but he didn’t want to ask straight out how they met. He decided to approach it from the day she had worked in the park. Having just mentioned the break in, the admission came out easily.

“Damn! Could you delete that bit? I never told Dad that.”

“I will leave it out of the statement. You can change things if I get it wrong. What do you think of Robbo and Thea?”

She admitted to being ambivalent, and only really deciding to go there because Wanda hadn’t answered.

“The reason I asked, is because I think your father wants them blamed for you getting snatched.”

“But they weren’t, were they?”

“That is what we are investigating.”

“They didn’t force me to go to them,” Abbie admitted. “But I’m glad I met Wanda on the way. I didn’t expect that.”

“Well, it seems like she has a knack for finding trouble.”

“Where is she?”

“Out on bail. Like Thea. Robbo is still in hospital, he was hurt badly by one of the abductors.”

“Do you mean that the police think they took me?”

“Were accomplices,” David corrected. “After all, Robbo and Thea were trying to get you on their side.”

Abbie fell silent.

David decided that he had enough. The least he had wanted was the timing of her movements, and as Abbie had just talked, he had managed to work that out. It was also good to have her view of what Robbo and Thea had done. They had been trying to protect her. Not all of that would be in the statement, at least at first. He could add more details later.

“Will my Dad be allowed to read my statement?” Abbie asked.

"He is your parent."

"Does he have to know I made one?"

"I expect he will think it important."

"Should he have been here?"

"Not necessarily. I asked the nurse to sit in, for the sake of propriety. Would you have preferred to have him here?"

"No!" Was her emphatic reply, and that told David a great deal.

David guessed Abbie was thinking that her father would raise hell when he discovered she had been questioned without him there. He decided on a bit of reassurance.

"The statement will be a simple run through of the basic facts," he said. "Bland, with no opinions."

"Okay."

"I will have the relevant parts transferred into legalese, and bring it back for you to sign before you go home." He gave her a reassuring grin.

"Will I be in trouble for running off?"

"The police won't press charges for that," David assured her. "I expect your parents might think differently."

Once again, David sensed her reluctance, through her abrupt clasping of forearms. He left her to her thoughts and thanked the nurse for being present.

"You will not mention what you heard, please," David asked her.

"No, sir. Naturally not."

"Thank you. Could I also have you sign a form to attest that you were present throughout the making of the statement?"

"Yes, certainly."

Once outside the private hospital, and when he was sure no one was close enough to over hear him, David called Kelso.

"David, Sir. I have confirmation that Carson may well have a mobile other than his registered one. No, I can't give you a number. Carson changed Abbie's phone and deleted numbers from the memory."

Kelso asked him to hold for a moment.

"That's not very helpful," Kelso challenged. "We have his phone records for his home phone and all the mobiles – his, his wife's' and Abbie's. None of them make a lot of calls."

"Surely that supports that he must have another mobile he uses for business," David insisted. "It's probably a prepaid phone."

"Do you have any tricks to find out that number?" Kelso challenged.

"One or two," David said cautiously. "No calls have come in to Carson yet?"

It was pretty well a rhetorical question, since they were hoping Carson would try something.

"Carson is getting downright edgy. His wife is clinging to him, not letting him leave. He escaped her for a while, by hiding in his office, but I think he will find an excuse to go out before long."

"Can you get the doctor to give them both a sleeping tablet? Or delay his going out for half an hour?"

"Why?"

"If he's going to try send a message, my guess is he will use a public wi-fi – like at the shopping centre. It will be closing in twenty minutes. It may mean he has to delay his attempt until morning."

"There are the fast food places that have free wi-fi too," Kelso pointed out.

"I know, but they are too open."

"What are you going to do?"

"I have to get back to the house, and I need to have a word with the police IT experts. I may have to adapt something to work here."

"When can you have your gadget ready?"

"Definitely by morning. Sooner preferably. When it's ready,

I will get there and sit outside. I have an app on my tablet that can pick up nearby wi-fi signals. We might get lucky."

Kelso told him to hop on it, and have Fred type Abbie's statement. David wasted no time getting back from the city. Part of his mind was on the details he needed to check with the local experts, but he was sure he would get something useful. He only ever admitted that the app, devised by Wanda's cousin, only deciphered the number destination of an incoming call, and that any subsequent message was scrambled. He always omitted to mention that it could also trace the call to the originating number. It was a very basic form of some highly sophisticated eavesdropping programs.

Several hours later, when he was in position outside Carson's house, he opened the app on his tablet and sent Kelso a text message saying he was ready.

During the night, one of the police IT experts, whose nickname was 'Gogo' watched the tablet while David had some sleep in the car. He was very interested in the technology, and asked a lot of questions. He was well prepared should a call come in while he was on watch.

David woke early, and confirmed that nothing significant had occurred. A record of all calls that were over a certain signal intensity had been recorded, but none had been directed at the Carson house, some might have originated from there or neighbouring houses.

"Carson may have been trying to reach Delaney," David suggested. "Were any numbers repeated?"

Three were pointed out, and David added them and the originating number to a list of numbers to trigger the program. It also triggered when the signal strength was over a certain level he had set when calibrating the program.

Gogo nudged him and nodded towards Carson's house. Carson wasn't quite running to his car, but he did back out faster than prudent. David noted the time. A little after seven. Some of the shops would be opening. He wondered what Carson's excuse was for going out, and leaving his wife with strangers at such a time. Anything he needed could have been fetched for him. Down the street, one of the unobtrusive unmarked cars, drove off after Carson. It reported Carson turning into the shopping centre, and David noted that time, and also the time when one of the occupants, now following him on foot, reported him entering the shops. When the man reached the doors, and threaded his way through the early shoppers, Carson had lost himself.

David quietly suggested that the man look for places where a person could be unobserved and make a phone call by playing a voice message into it. Almost right away, a call triggered his program. Again he noted the time. He had Gogo message Kelso, "Messaging now."

The choice of going to the shopping centre might have been Carson trying to trick people into thinking he wanted a few groceries or a paper. Or the real reason maybe to use the free wi-fi. He wondered how tech savvy Carson was. One question he'd snuck in on Abbie was whether her father received a lot of calls. She'd said no, but when he was working at home he made lots of calls or was on his computer.

David considered how a scam artist, such as he believed Carson to be, would work. If he knew about burner phones, he might change his number frequently, but somehow, David tended to think he wouldn't. If he was grooming prospects to invest, they would need to be able to contact him, or be called back. A constant number change would be suspicious.

When the message finished, he noted the time, and the call length, and mentally counted seconds until Carson was spotted going into the supermarket. He also counted the time from when Carson came out of the supermarket with some groceries, and when he emerged into the carpark. Maybe the timing could be used to work out where Carson had stopped, to make the call. He can't have gone in far, and maybe the shopkeepers could be quizzed, or security cameras checked.

David tried to ping the phone number he had decoded, but Carson must have turned the phone off. Maybe he guessed the police might try calling the number back. He growled in frustration. Back home in California, he had access to high powered phone interception gear and a useful group of tech geeks.

It was also frustrating that he had to work according to the police allowed practices. He wasn't allowed to hack into the CCTV cameras, in the shopping centre. Kelso would have to request permission.

When the relief officers took over from Kelso and his crew, Kelso came and joined David in the car.

"Carson put on an Oscar worthy performance," he said. "He asked if anyone outside saw someone watching for him to go out. He wanted to ask questions of the bastard."

David smiled grimly. Carson had that angle thought out. "What did he come back with?"

"Chocolate and iced tea, to calm his wife when she woke up, and a newspaper."

"What did you pick up inside?" David asked.

"The call came from a mobile, through the tower at the shopping centre," Kelso reported. "Did you get more?"

"Yes. I got the number the call came from, and the destination number. Did you try ringing back?"

Kelso nodded. "It had been turned off."

"I tried to ping it and found the same." David went on to mention the timing and his idea to check for potential witnesses. "Too bad you can't just search him."

Kelso growled. "He's a slimy piece."

"Best I can do now is monitor that particular number — the one that called. It was used during the night three times. He must be getting mad at Delaney for not answering. Are you going to have the recording of the voice analysed?"

"I doubt it will help. It sounds like it was done with a text to voice program, as you suggested. Best we can hope for is to try to analyse the background noise."

"Okay, I think you need to keep Carson off balance, so he will forget to erase that message he sent."

Kelso grinned maliciously. "He might have just tossed the recording device, but I don't think he will yet. He may need it again. I think I did rattle him. I mentioned we were getting search warrants for all the storage units, and our reasoning. In truth, I already have the contact details of the hires, and have been in contact with the majority. Most allowed us to record their verbal agreement to us looking inside.”

A tone alerted David. “That phone is active again.” He scribbled down the destination number and tower, the time of call and the length. He showed Kelso the number.

“That’s the number for the manager of the units,” Kelso said, well pleased. He dialled the number himself, and David heard part of the conversation, and listened as Kelso repeated, Joe Stillman, PO Box 58, Bellfield East. Got that. What did Stillman say?” Kelso listened, and finally ended the call.

David waited for Kelso to speak. “Mr Stillman, apparently, just received the message I sent out on Friday. He claims he will be out of this area until next week. He asked the manager to use the master key to check nothing in his unit has been disturbed. He has no problem with the police eyeballing the contents, but only from the doorway. He does not want his confidential records looked at.”

David tried to ping the number again, and again the phone was off.

“I don’t think we can hold off reporting Abbie has been found for much longer,” Kelso decided. “Do you think the girl will mention how long she’d been at the hospital?”

“I can’t be sure. She didn’t make an issue of when they would come in. That’s all I can say.”

“I don’t know that we can get much more here. When you heard the call come in, was exactly when we had it inside. So it is very likely he made the call, but I don’t know if we have enough to pull him in. That Stillman name is probably false, but I will have it run through the system anyway.”

“Do you want me to keep monitoring here?” David asked.

“No. Gogo, are you happy to stay on duty for a while longer?”

“Fine by me,” the IT expert agreed.

“Will you drive the car back when you finish up?” David asked.

“Sure, mate.”

Kelso gestured to David to get out, and they went to his car.

"How are you going to play finding Abbie?"

"I'll check with Des, but the simpler the better. We can say we spotted Delaney or one of his mates, followed them back to some building, went in and found the girl. We don't have to give precise details, even though the media ghouls will want them. Maybe they will be satisfied filming the happy homecoming. "Either way, there will need to be a delay between the report, and Carson getting there – after all, she would need to be checked over, asked some questions, have a chance to have a shower."

"I will leave all that to you."

"You should check up on your own problem patient," Kelso suggested.

"She's already texted me. She won't be allowed out until the doctor has seen her again, but she has permission to have a few minutes with Robbo before she leaves the hospital. It is a good thing they are not at the same hospital as Abbie."

"I will have Fred there to pick her up, unless you want to be there?"

"In other circumstances, yes, I would. However, I have to be careful not to be seen to be too involved with her."

Chapter 4

Annie grabbed the morning paper before her father even had a chance to look at the headlines. Late the previous night, she had received a text from David. All the message said was, "Martin is okay. Please don't try to talk to him."

Even though it was a relief, it made her worry more. Was Martin in trouble? It was any indication of that which she was looking for, rather than news about Abbie. There was nothing. Just an article that was a plea from Abbie's parents for news of their daughter.

That had confused her. Why didn't they know she was safe? Kelly had said they would be told. She wished she could discuss it with someone, but there must have been an impelling reason why the Carson's were still in the dark.

"Still no news?" her father asked, pointedly.

"No," Annie said, truthfully. "Here's your paper."

Lucky-pup was yapping to be let out and fed, so Annie went to see to her. Cuddling her dog, and telling her how clever she was, was the nearest she could come to talking about things.

While the little dog, who had already grown to twice her original size, was inhaling her food, Hank Jamieson called from the kitchen.

"Were you going to visit Maude Hartley today?"

"Oh, yes. But I haven't heard from Wanda. She might not be available. Naomi said she would come with me if I wanted to go."

"Why don't you send a text message to Wanda or David?"

"They might be busy."

"Well, if they are, they will answer when they can. It is less intrusive than a phone call."

Annie saw the sense in that, she didn't want to interrupt their work. She made her message short, and went to get her own breakfast.

It wasn't until she was nearly finished that a reply came. It came from Wanda's number, but it was David who answered. "Sorry, Wanda and I are both tied up on another matter. You and Naomi can visit Maude. Ring first to let the place know. David." A second text came with the number.

That was the trouble with adults, Annie decided. They had other stuff to do and couldn't always be available. Like her parents now. But mostly, until she was in high school, one or other had been around. Wanda and David had their own kids to return to. They would want to get their job here finished.

So she decided to call Naomi, only to discover that she was at Bunnings, helping at the scout's sausage sizzle.

"Dad, can I walk up to the shops? Naomi and the scouts are doing a sausage sizzle fund-raiser."

"Maybe I should come too. A sausage with onion sounds mighty appetizing. I guess they are working to raise money for the building project. I might even shout you one too."

"Okay!" Annie agreed promptly, making it sound like she was agreeing because of the food offer, rather than that she was having second thoughts about going on her own. Kelly's direction, two days before, to stay at home, may still be valid.

Her father did as promised, and after eating his sausage and complementing the cooks, wandered off to browse in the hardware shop. Naomi, in between customers, had a chance to chat.

"I'm only on until twelve. Karen was here earlier, but had to do something with her mum. She'll be free after that. We could all go and visit Maude. I can see if Dad will drive us."

"Or mine might," Annie suggested. "Wanda was going to come, but something came up."

"Is she helping to find Abbie?"

"I don't think so," Annie hedged. "But they came here on

other business."

"But she was helping Maude, wasn't she?" Naomi countered. "So she is into helping people."

"She's not stuffy like a lot of grownups," Annie agreed. "She admitted that when she was our age she was put in a girls training centre."

Naomi's eyebrows rose. "Did she say what for?"

"Only that being there meant she had somewhere to sleep and didn't have to steal food."

"Makes me glad I have a really good dad," Naomi murmured as another group of hungry people converged on the cook tent.

Annie moved out of the way and watched the people coming and going. She spotted her Dad talking to someone, and some unwelcome but familiar faces. Unfortunately, the appetising smell attracted them.

"Well, well, Jamieson and Baxter," Tom Logan said genially. "How about a free sausage for a friend?"

"What? Spent all your pocket money already?" Naomi said with a grin. "Tell you what, you come back with $3.50 and we will give you the pick of the cooked sausages, and your choice of extras, and even throw in a drink for you."

The people who were waiting politely began to grin, more so when it seemed that the two boys didn't realise that she had quoted them a price a dollar higher that what was listed on the board. They waited until the boys had stalked off before laughing and complementing Naomi on her handling of them. Some even put their change into the donations jar.

In the next lull, Naomi said to Annie, "You know, I used to think those two were okay. Now I don't know what Gail and co see in them."

"A supposedly rich step-dad," Annie suggested, as her Dad came up with Baxter. One of the other parents, soon told him how well his daughter had handled the hecklers.

"Maybe the scouts should canvas the local businesses for

donations towards fitting out the new building?" Hank Jamieson suggested. "Perhaps even the locals themselves."

"You know those two, do you?" Baxter asked his daughter.

"They go to our school," she said.

"Weren't they two of those that got into trouble?"

"Yeah, but they were only suspended. They are back again now."

"They know that young Martin?" Baxter asked.

"Cousins of his," Annie inserted.

"I heard them saying something about an ambulance at his place yesterday," Baxter said with concern, "and Police still being around, watching his place."

Naomi glanced at Annie, brows raised questioningly.

Annie managed to say, "I wouldn't listen to them. They like to make trouble for Martin. Probably only heard part of something and made up the rest. What is your opinion of Martin, Mr Baxter?"

"Quite a presentable and willing to help young man," Baxter said immediately.

"Exactly. Martin and I suggested they could help with the clear out, but neither of them deigned to get their hands dirty," Annie said.

Baxter began to chuckle. "I wonder if they became like that because if their names?"

"What do you mean, Dad?"

Annie saw her father grinning too. He suggested, "Do a Google search on the names and see what comes up. Anyway, Annie, what have you decided to do?"

"Ah, I am going to ring up and see if we can visit Maude later. This arvo sometime. We're going to see if Karen wants to come too."

"What's this?" Baxter asked.

Annie explained.

"Well, I could drop you off. I would like to tell her how our plans are coming along. She is our patron. All things considered,

I can't see how she could ever have been how people said."

"She is really nice, Mr Baxter," Annie said. "And she needs friends. You should come."

"Okay, Annie. I will."

A knock on his office door caused Jeremy Carson to blank his computer screen and check his desk.

"Come in!"

Kelso entered quietly. "Your daughter has been found. She will be okay. She has been taken to the hospital to be checked over."

Carson stood abruptly. "I want to see her!"

"Naturally. However, I have suggested to your wife that a change of clothes is needed for your daughter. The police will likely want to test her clothing for indicators of where she has been."

"What do you mean?" Carson seemed alarmed.

"That is what I was told, sir," Kelso claimed. "However, I was under the belief that the place where she was found, had been checked only yesterday. She was probably kept somewhere else."

"Well, where was she?"

"Sir, now that I am no longer an active police officer, I don't get told everything."

"What about the bastard..."

"Who took her?" Kelso suggested the rest of the question. "That's where the police had some luck."

The expression on Carson's face changed, to one of avid interest. "Delaney was spotted and took off. The officers went into the building he had come from."

"Did they find my money?"

"If they did, it may be required for evidence," Kelso countered.

Carson abruptly strode from his office. "What's taking Victoria so long?"

Kelso moved so he could give the office an intense scrutiny before following. He hadn't expected to see a voice recorder in plain view, and didn't. He didn't have authority to search the room, either.

The housekeeper went upstairs at Carson's direction.

"You'll be able to remove all this then." Carson gestured to laptop computers and the lines attached to his phone.

"Although it is unlikely that Delaney will call if he realises that we have your daughter, it might be wise to keep it here until we get him. It is only a matter of time."

Abbie was glad to have had time to herself before having her parents descend on her. She'd had time to think and decide what to tell her father. However, she was a little confused – she had lost a day somewhere. She had spent the past night in the hospital, and had been told her parents would be in that morning. Somehow though, she had the feeling that her parents wouldn't be told until today. That too was confusing, since surely there were worried sick about her. She admitted to herself that she hoped her father was. He would be livid if he knew she'd been here overnight, and been questioned already. So she was going to act like she was still confused. Certainly, she would not be admitting how much she had told the good looking guy who had taken her statement, and hoped he would only stick to the facts like he said.

She didn't want to get Robbo and Thea in trouble. They hadn't taken her, and she hadn't known of the restraining order. Whoever had taken her must have something against her father.

She was sitting on the remade bed, in a borrowed dressing gown, when she heard her mother.

"Abbie, Darling!"

She hopped off the bed and raced at her. It felt really good, to have her mother hugging so tightly.

"Oh, my darling girl, are you alright? No one interfered with you did they?"

"No, mum. They said I'm fine. Did you bring me some clothes? They took mine to do tests on or something."

That distracted Victoria Carson from her dramatics. She took the bag her husband was carrying. He was standing aloof from his wife and daughter.

"They put you in a ward," Carson observed.

"It was so I could have privacy," Abbie said dismissively, glad the bed had been made, so it would seem true when she said, "And if I felt like it I could lie down while I waited for you. Daddy, can I go home? I want to have my stuff around me."

"We will need to collect what you had at the hotel. Why don't you go and get cleaned up and dressed?"

"They let me use the shower," Abbie told him.

"Well make yourself presentable. Unfortunately, it seems the media have heard about you being found. I don't want you talking to them."

Carson turned as someone knocked on the door behind him. "Who are you?"

David knew Carson recognised him. However, he introduced himself using his Task Force persona, and noted Carson's lips go thin and tight. "I was in earlier to get some details from your daughter. While events were fresh. I need her to sign the statement."

"Shouldn't I or my wife been present for that?" Carson demanded.

"I assure you, Mr Carson, I had a female member of the staff present during the short interview. As Michael Delaney was recognised as one of the abductors, the Task Force is working with the local police."

"I want to see what my daughter has told you."

"I will need her to read it over first. It has been translated into what I term 'legalese'. You may need to help decipher it to be sure it's what she means. However, as I said, I need her to read it first."

Carson didn't push further. He decided to switch topics.

"So Delaney was caught. Where exactly?"

David played innocent. "It was local to your residence, that's all I know. I am not greatly familiar with this area." His accent seemed to confirm that statement.

"What's going to happen to the bastard?"

"He is to go before a judge. New charges have been added to those he is already facing. Bail will be refused, and he is to be kept at the maximum security remand centre."

David would have loved to have had Wanda with him to see if she could pick up what Carson was thinking. He had near perfect control of his facial expression. That he was thinking lots of thoughts was only betrayed by a faint muscle twitch.

After a few moments, he asked, "There were others involved. What about them?"

"The police are questioning a number of people. Only one has yet to be found."

"The people staying at the house?" Carson insisted.

"The man hasn't been able to be questioned," David said, truthfully. "He is still in a serious condition. Delaney stabbed him in the abdomen when he tried to stop him taking your daughter."

David decided that it was a risk to mention it, but likely Abbie would insist Robbo and Thea weren't involved. Carson might have to rethink his demands about them.

The tightening of Carson's jaw became even more pronounced.

To himself, David thought, I hope he is thinking of what Delaney might have done to Abbie.

As an echo to that thought, a now dressed Abbie was emerging from the room's en-suite.

"Mum, I don't want make-up. They told me not to use it until the grazes are better. No one is going to expect me to look like I was going out to the opera or anything."

Victoria was hovering with a comb in hand.

Abbie saw David and came over. "Oh. Do you need me to sign that statement?"

"Yes, Miss Carson," he said formally. "It has been put in the form the local police needed. You will need to read over everything carefully to make sure it is correct."

"Okay."

David slipped the documents from a folder. "You will need to sign all three copies where indicated. One copy is for you to keep."

"Will Abigail need to testify in court?" Victoria asked, frowning with concern.

"I don't believe it will be necessary as we have a witness who could identify Michael Delaney as being there."

"Who? That other woman who was there?" Carson was back to being belligerent.

Abbie took the moment of his being distracted to scan read the statement, and sighed with relief.

"Yes," David said tersely, as if it was a subject he wanted to avoid. Carson's faint smile told David that he knew who the person was, even if the paper had not mentioned names. He would have confirmation when he contrived to read the statement, as he was edging into a position behind his daughter to do. Still, he would only read the name, Wanda, without a surname.

Maybe, contemplating his own vendetta with the low life who had chummied up to his daughter would further distract him from ditching evidence. He must be dying to accuse him, a member of the Task Force, of having criminals working for them.

As Abbie reached around for a pen, Carson finished reading. "You're a damn fool, you know." His tone sounded mild, but likely he would say a lot more when he got home.

David pitied the girl, but Kelso had told him they had no

reason to take her from her parents. Carson had better remember that Abbie might up again and leave if he got too overbearing.

"Do you know what my father would have done to me if I'd done what you've done?" Carson roared when he had made Abbie sit down in the family room. "He'd have taken off his belt and made sure I couldn't sit down for a week."

Abbie saw her father's hand twitching towards belt, and she could almost feel the pain already.

"Jeremy," Victoria interrupted, "Don't you think she has been through enough?"

"No! I want to make sure she's not going to be such a fool again. They are going to think she is no better than a whore if she runs off after every boy who flaunts his charms. She could have been raped, or worse. Then who would ever want to marry her? She might have been killed."

The chair was not nearly big enough to disappear into. Being rolled up in that smelly blanket had been horrible. Feeling that man's hands moving over it, terrifying. His leering threats had made her skin crawl.

Right now, though, her father was worse than all she'd endured and she had no option but to listen to the horrible things he was saying. She put her fingers in her ears to block it out, but her hands were savagely yanked away.

"You will listen to me! I can't afford to neglect my business just because of a damn fool. So, you and I will have a contract. Understand?"

Abbie only dared a nod. She'd agree to anything. Just to get him to shut up.

"First, you run off again – don't bother coming back. You know how horrible the world can be now, so if you go, it must be because you want more of it. Don't make me regret rescuing you from that orphanage. Agreed?"

Abbie nodded. It was the only sane option.

"Next, you're going to work your butt off for the rest of this year. If you get into any more trouble there, I'll be pulling you out and sending you to the local church high school."

His blazing eyes seemed to pierce right into her and she shivered.

"I am going to be keeping track of you – where you go, who you see, who you talk to, what you do online – until I am sure I can trust you to have sense. And finally, when I tell you to do, or not do something, you will obey me, exactly, immediately, or you will feel my hand on your back side."

"Jeremy," Victoria tried to intercede.

"I'm finished. Go! Get out of my sight. Don't come out of your room except for school, meals, and bathroom needs. No, Victoria. You stay here."

Abbie couldn't leave fast enough. She wanted to scream, "I hate you!" but her father would hit her if she did. She knew it.

Her room was tidier than she had left it, and right now, the addition of extra pillows on her bed, and an unfamiliar throw rug, was an invitation to hide there. She didn't stop to think who had put them there, or who had tidied her room, she just dived out of sight, and erupted into tears.

When she finally stopped, the thought did occur to her. Surely, her mother hadn't had a chance to. They had gone from the hospital to the hotel and then straight home.

A soft knock caught her attention.

"Go away!"

"Miss Carson, I have your things from that place in Footscray."

"Oh. I'm sorry. You can come in."

Mrs Buttrose had a plastic bag in one hand, and her backpack in the other.

"Where did you get this stuff? Does my obnoxious father know?"

"It was delivered shortly before you got back. A rather

presentable young man brought it."

"Did he give his name?"

"David, Miss. He left his card for you."

"It must be the guy who took my statement. Does his horridness know you are giving it to me?"

"Naturally. He checked your phone to ensure it still worked."

Abbie held her tongue. That would not have been his reason.

"Thank you," Abbie said after a moment. She hoped the housekeeper might prove to be an ally.

"I will come up later and see if you would like some hot milk."

"Thanks."

As soon as she was alone again, Abbie grabbed the plastic bag and took out her phone. It was going to need charging, but it was on. She checked the messages, all had been read even the ones that had come while...she was in hell. Her father had no right! She began to read them, but after two of Gail's snide texts, she just deleted all messages. No wonder her father had left them. He probably thought she deserved to be punished by her friends too.

Her tablet, which she took from her bag, was flat. Had her father tried to look there too? The charger was also in her pack so she plugged it in. No doubt Gail and the others would have been all over Facebook too.

As soon as she had minimum charge, she looked, deciding she ought to be prepared for the worst.

All the messages from Gail, Helen and Clare were immediately deleted. She glanced at those from other people she knew and they ranged from downright rude, to positively crude. They went too.

There was one from Adam. "Seriously, Abs, there's something wrong with you."

"He can't talk," she snarled quietly.

Only one didn't make her want to immediately delete it. The

one from Fairydust. Annie simply said, "I'm glad you are safe back. Are you ok?"

Tears returned to her already sore eyes. She replied with a smiley face wearing dark glasses, and, "Thanks for sending me your class notes."

She didn't want to put anything more than that on Facebook or even in a text from her phone. Too bad she had lost the new one somewhere. She would ring that nice David guy and ask, but she didn't dare.

Maybe Annie would let me use hers to ring, when she was back at school. That thought made her feel sick.

Gail wouldn't be restrained by having to type her comments, would probably want all the horrid details so she could torment her over and over, and would be telling everyone that she had faked her own abduction.

Annie wouldn't, a little voice in her head said. Annie had found her, somehow. Her and the little dog. Would she be bragging about that? No. Somehow, she didn't think she would.

Abbie found an internet news site and read a few articles from that day. And some from the previous days. It felt odd, reading about herself, but all articles made it seem that the police had found her. All but one of the group had been caught.

It was her fault that Wanda was in more trouble, Abbie realised, after seeing her in a picture taken in Footscray. They thought she was involved. Her father did, he'd mentioned her in part of his tirade. How had he even known about her, except from reading her statement? She had been friendly enough, and cared about seeing her out late on her own. She hadn't been all lecturing about it though.

It had been stupid, running off, because she thought her father was using her for something crooked. Meeting Wanda had been a real fluke of luck. The lewd suggestions from various men who'd been lounging around, had been giving her shivers before that. For some reason, fewer men made crude advances once Wanda was around.

She still resented her father and his dogmatic 'contract', but what could she do? Her attempts to get away had been abysmal failures. She would just have to do what he said, there was no other option.

Episode 21

Adding Pieces Together

Chapter 1

One advantage of her paramedic training, Wanda decided, was that she could read most of her chart and understand what everything meant. That, and knowing how much better she felt, provided her enough reason for to insist on being discharged. The doctor might argue, but she had things she needed to do.

That doctor had better hurry up, she thought as her watch told her the morning was almost over. It wasn't much later when he arrived and picked up her chart to read.

"Well, you seem to have recovered from the blood loss," he told her. "Though I would like to have you rest in here for another day to recover further."

"I'm fine. I have things I have to do."

"Mrs Davis, you are not fine! The scans we did after you were brought in last night, have shown that the little bones in the ear that vibrate with sound, were damaged by the blow you received. You need to have an operation to fix the problem, or you risk being deaf in that ear."

The news sent a shiver down her spine, even as she realised that must have been the reason David's receiver bead hadn't seemed to work.

"You need to be aware that such an injury may affect your balance. You should not try to climb anything higher than your bed."

"That's no fun," she muttered, allowing droll humour to distract her.

"No," the doctor agreed. "However, I contacted an ear specialist and he tells me that it should be possible to operate and realign the bones. Being young and otherwise in good health – usually – they should fuse back together and your hearing will return."

"So I am going to be back to normal then? Able to climb a ladder if I need to?"

"He believes so."

"When can I see him?"

"He will be here tonight and will be able to fit you into his theatre schedule tomorrow."

"What time tonight?"

"Between six and seven. That is why I think it's best to stay here and rest.'

"No. I have things I need to do. I can be back here tonight?"

The doctor looked at her and considered. "Your arm wound has been repaired. If you break the stitches, you are likely to cause tissue damage and the arm's function may be impaired."

"I'll be good," Wanda promised.

"I will have that arm well strapped before you leave," the doctor countered.

"So you will let me out?"

"You won't be discharged, but if you promise not to overuse that arm, or try climbing, you will be allowed to leave and return at 6 pm."

"That'll do," Wanda agreed.

She was already dressing in her spare clothes, dropped in for her during the night, when the nurse came in with a trolley of equipment. Even though she understood the reason, having her upper arm immobilised and requiring a sling to support it, was annoying and made her feel vulnerable.

The nurse helped her to finish getting dressed in the loose clothing. Then, before she went out, she called Commander Britten, and asked if he had received permission for her to talk to Robbo Mainwright. He had, and he told her to speak to the ward sister. That was easy. She was in the same ward, and was told she could have ten minutes, but not to stress him.

Having little time and no inclination to play word games, she got straight to the point. At least he was awake, and recognised her.

"I have given the police a statement that Abbie went to you of her own free will. It was damn stupid of you to ring Carson to needle him. He has that call recorded."

She didn't let the invalid retort. "Thea has been charged as an accessory to kidnapping, and for breaking the terms of Carson's restraining order, but I don't think that will stand up in the end. She has been allowed bail, and when she is bailed out will be allowed to stay where I am staying."

"Where's that? The local park?" Robbo said weakly.

Wanda merely grinned at his feeble attempt to dominate her. "No! Now listen! As soon as you are deemed well enough, you will be questioned and required to make a statement. Stick to the events from when Abbie and I arrived, to when you lost the plot. If they ask your connection to Carson, say it is a civil matter. All they can charge you with, is what Thea is facing. It seems that Carson hasn't reported a few break-ins at his house, but he has been trying to implicate you further in Abbie's abduction."

"That bastard!"

"Save it, Robbo. He is also mistakenly trying to blame me, and since you have been here since that night, I am a likelier candidate. Just be as close as you possibly can to citing the correct times when things happened, okay?"

Robbo nodded once. "Who are you? You aren't acting like before."

"No, but I have a few questions I need you to answer."

"Are you a policeman?"

"No."

"Then why should I tell you anything?"

"Okay, let's say you give me a yes or no answer to two questions?"

"Maybe."

"Have you heard of the name Jacob Hillier?"

Robbo jerked, and then grimaced. "Did Thea mention him?"

Wanda shook her head. "I came across the name in relation to another inquiry, and it was linked to Carson. So, I take that as a yes. What about Jason Dell Walton?"

This time Robbo shook his head. "No. Who are you?"

"Something like a private investigator doing a background check on Carson. So, when you get out on bail, get in touch with my partner. I will leave his card. I think it will be to your benefit to share what you know."

"What's in this for you? Who's paying you?"

"Satisfaction and no one. You may not be the only two people Carson has shafted. The people I want to help, well, I think they suffered worse."

The nurse came in to shoo her out, but Wanda left one of Kelso's cards in his bedside drawer.

From there, Wanda had gone to the Melbourne custody centre and did what was needed to get Thea Mainwright out on bail.

Thea emerged, looking bewildered, perhaps expecting the impossible presence of her brother. Wanda went up to her.

"You? You got me out?"

"You arguing?" Wanda spoke with a trace of her rogue persona.

"No, but...why? And what happened to you?"

"Most of this was from the other night. It's nothing you need worry about."

"How do you know my brother?"

"I was with Abbie Carson when she was doing community service and he came to talk to her."

"Is she a friend of yours?"

"I was hoping to become one, but....things happened."

"Have they found Abbie?"

"Not that I have heard on the news," Wanda said, which was the truth. "But I can tell you that Robbo has been down listed to merely 'in danger'."

That really brought a change to Thea. "Will they let me see him?"

"We can find out, but if they do, it won't be for long. They only gave me ten minutes."

"You went to see him?"

"Yes. I am hoping to trade information with him."

"What about?"

"A mutual person of interest. Jeremy Carson. I am doing a background check on him for someone."

"Well, from what Robbo has told me, he's not eligible for an OA."

"What?" Wanda had to ask.

"A medal. The Order of Australia," Thea clarified.

"Oh! How much do you know about him?"

"Some, but Robbo has said to keep it close. Not to spread it. We don't want him to be warned."

"No worries there, for now," Wanda agreed. Robbo had told her enough to go on with. "Come on. I have a car and driver waiting outside."

As they neared Fred's car, Wanda said, "This is our ride. The driver is Fred, a retired policeman. I am keeping him amused with my comings and goings. His reaction when he sees you should be fun."

While no longer spiked up, Thea's hair was still a vivid

purple.

Fred's mouth did gape open until Thea asked, "Will it be possible to get stuff from the house?"

"Do you really want to go back there?"

"Not really. But all I have is there."

"Fred, can you find out?" Wanda requested. A nod was her answer. "You can borrow some of my stuff if you want to change."

Thea gave a grateful nod. She was still wearing the old clothes she had been sleeping in.

Wanda decided that she wasn't surprised that Annie still came to visit Maude, but seeing the third girl, and Mr Baxter, was a pleasant surprise. It would be good if the scouts took an interest in her. Still, it was a complication. She didn't want to face questions from Annie. There was little that she was at liberty to discuss.

David had helped her put a dark rinse through her hair, and some of the make-up, since the police doctor had ensured her arm was strapped to keep her from being used too much. How good her disguise was, she would have to see. Tyrell though, had been warned to expect a stranger.

The bandaged arm and ear were a good distraction to an on-looker, when as her 'rogue' persona, she was still being held on kidnapping and breaking charges. It was all misdirection.

Tyrell arrived at the same time as the girls and Baxter were signing in, and when she rose, he came over.

Annie saw him, recognised him and looked hopefully in Wanda's direction. Her expression didn't change, and Wanda breathed easier. The disguise was working. The Trustee, though, looked concerned.

"I thought this was just for show," he said quietly, as he gestured for her to sit first. "But you look…"

"David used too much make-up," Wanda said quietly to cut him off.

He nodded, getting the message, and waited until Maude's visitors had gone further into the building before asking, "Are you going to tell me what is going on?"

"Did you defer the meeting with Carson?" Wanda asked.

"Yes, naturally. We wanted to meet the girl, but it seems she is still missing."

"I am allowed to assure you that the girl is safe. However, we don't think we have picked up everyone involved, so as yet, her parents are still suffering agonies of guilt and worry."

"That seems a rather heartless attitude."

"For Victoria Carson, maybe," Wanda admitted. "For Jeremy Carson, he deserves it."

Tyrell stared at her. "I had the police and the Department of Human Services check him out," he protested. "They had nothing against him."

"That only means he has been diabolically clever," Wanda said. "In his outraged parent persona, he is demanding that two people who served him with papers for a civil suit, be charged with the kidnap."

"I heard a group of people were taken into custody," Tyrell revealed.

"What you didn't hear, was that I was one of them."

Now Tyrell stared, just managing not to gape.

"It's true, and it's deliberate," Wanda assured him. "I kind of went off the radar for a while, and I was illegally recording certain conversations. Carson discovered that I was. So when he was told that his first two suspects had at worst just encouraged Abbie to go to them, and couldn't have abducted her, I became the ring leader. I had contrived to meet Abbie during a stint of community service. In fact, I failed to protect her from being taken. I did recognise the leader of those who broke into the house, and it was mutual. Mickey Delaney."

Tyrell repeated the name, disgust in his voice.

Wanda nodded. "So to cut this story short, I believe Carson told Delaney where he believed Abbie had gone, had already arranged a place where she could be taken, a storage unit leased in the name of one of those accusing him of things. Then, for whatever perverse reason, Mickey didn't take her there. Probably he decided to tighten the screws on Carson who had agreed to pay him 50 thousand dollars for services performed over a decade ago, that was part of an investment, soon to mature.”

“My God!” Tyrell exclaimed, still softly. “Can you prove this?”

“The police are building a case. The timing of various events will be one crucial element. In my ‘rogue’ persona, I can be questioned on what I overheard, when I was illegally in his house, even if the recording can’t be used. And I have, a very good memory.”

“But what caused that silly girl to run off?”

“Abbie was listening to her parent’s talking, and her father said, ‘After this, we will never have to work again.’ She was already suspecting he was up to something shady.”

“Is he after the Hartley fortune?”

“That’s our contention.”

“So what should I do?”

“For now, delay a bit. Abbie will be ‘found’ soon, but we hope that a particular person will take a certain kind of action to try and pressure the police.”

“I think I can guess who that might be,” Tyrell murmured. “I am going to need proof. The Trustees agreed to make the girl’s father a nominee on her trust, until she is 18. That is assuming the DNA tests pan out. I was hoping to get an impression of both the girl and her father yesterday.”

“Keep an open mind,” Wanda advised. “But stall the process. The police will advise you of any new information about Carson.”

“I still find it hard to believe,” Tyrell admitted.

“In all fairness, I would have to admit we might be wrong. However, I am certain of my belief. Carson is clever, and pays attention to details, but I think I have put him on the defensive, and on one point, he may assume something and not realise the abyss under his feet.”

“What started you checking him out?”

“The people who began the civil suit against him, claim to be his children, and claim he took off with their mother’s sizable inheritance, the money in all their accounts, and sold their house from around them. I still need to speak to both of those two, but the man was stabbed by Delaney, and is still in a very serious condition, and the girl won't talk without him."

"Do you know, that I also had you checked out?" Tyrell admitted. "I wondered why you had become involved with Maude."

"And?"

"And I can only conclude that some angel was looking after her."

"Let me guess? Commander Britten said, she is good at what she does, is too lucky by half, deserves to be locked up, and he hates damn Mavericks."

"Close. He said, 'thank god I have her working for me'. But I do think I will have to believe you can read minds."

Wanda shrugged. "Maybe I am just a good guesser. However, I would like some information to work on. I spoke to Maude a few days ago and made some notes I wanted to follow up on. She gave me some letters, the ones we found at the scout house, that were special to her. I read some."

"Go on with your questions. I will tell you if it is something I can't answer."

Chapter 3

Wanda went straight to the point. "When did you create the trust for Maude?"

"Virtually as soon as she was born. Her brothers had trust funds too. They took them over when they turned 21. When we realised that Maude was simple, we added extra clauses. And some more when she was old enough for boys to be interested in her."

"I understand both her brothers died. What happened to their estates?"

"Neither had wives or children, so the remaining capital returned to the family trust. If they had been survived by a wife, a portion would have gone to her. If there had been children, the remaining capital would be placed in a trust, or trusts, for them."

"So when Gerald and Charles died, their capital went back to their parents?"

"That's right."

"What happened when Maude had Timothy?"

Tyrell tensed. "How did you learn about him?"

Wanda told him and added, "And I spoke to Maude about him when I was here last."

"Did she mention who the father was?"

"Is there a reason you need to know?"

"I'd like to have words with him, yes. Taking advantage of a simple, grieving..."

Wanda leant over and touched his arm with her still usable hand. "I had the distinct impression that Timothy's father was taken advantage of by Maude."

"What?"

"Shh! Maude said she wanted a baby for her mum and pa."

Tyrell subsided and looked away. Finally, he turned back.

"When Gerald died, leaving Maude sole heir to the Hartley fortune, lots of lads started visiting her. Her parents were quite shocked when she announced she was pregnant. However, when she had the boy, they were overjoyed. They wanted the Hartley name to continue."

"So you would have started a trust for him?"

"What are you getting at?"

"I'm not sure. I am trying to figure out why Mickey Delaney wanted Maude put away for good."

Tyrell said, sombrely, "He discovered, that if she died, he would get nothing."

"Take a step back, will you? Did you start a trust for Timothy?"

"Yes, and Maude's parents insisted that we change the terms of her trust. Her husband would only get a stipend from the trust if she had children. He would not have any control."

Wanda nodded. It had proved to be a wise decision. "How did Timothy die?"

"SIDS," Tyrell said tersely. "Maude wasn't blamed. She was living with her parents and there was a nurse to help her."

"Okay, what happened to Timothy's trust?"

"It was wound up and absorbed into Maude's."

"Moving ahead. When Maude had the girls, you began trusts for them."

"Yes, and they are still active. We had to assume that the girls were still alive, even though we had lost track of them."

"When did you realise they were gone?"

"Not until she was arrested for kidnapping," Tyrell's expression was bleak. "Delaney seemed quite pleasant while he and Maude were going together. He told us that the Department had taken them because Maude wasn't able to look after them, and he couldn't because he had to work."

"What did you do about it?"

"Mr King, my superior, tried to find them, but the department claimed to know nothing about them. Delaney sent them somewhere out of spite, I think. I did tell him that the Hartley trust would have paid to have the girls looked after. He claimed, not to have known to contact us."

"Did he know about the girls' trusts?"

"Maude might have told him, but I am not sure. I did mention them to him when asking their whereabouts. I also mentioned the terms."

"How did he take it?"

"The obnoxious man just asked how much they were worth. Then he said the girls were better off in state care, because their mother almost drowned them at bath time."

"I really detest that man," Wanda said intensely.

"Do you think that someone is trying to muscle in on the trust account? Is that why you suggested the DNA test?"

"Yes, and her divorcing Mickey," Wanda confirmed. "One last question. If by chance, or chicanery, Maude's daughter or daughters come forward and claim their trusts, and Maude dies, what's the situation?"

Tyrell gave that notion some thought. "I hadn't thought that far. It was quite a shock, having someone who might be Gabrielle Hartley show up. However, assuming both were alive, at this time they would be minors. Their guardian might have to be a nominee. The guardian might get a small stipend. The children would get an allowance until they were of age and could take over control of their trust. The nominee would have access to a great deal of money. Woman, you have a horribly devious mind."

"Unfortunately true. Maybe the wording about the nominee should be modified to 'a nominee appointed by yourselves'?"

"I will certainly talk to Mr King about that. Do you think this business about finding the child's body is related?"

Wanda met his gaze. "My gut says yes, but I don't think the timing of the find was premeditated. Didn't the council take over the house and land because of unpaid rates?"

"It did, but that was all sorted out and Maude agreed to let the scouts have the house."

"That find might have precipitated the maturation date of the investment," Wanda suggested. "That might work in our favour. Now, changing topics. Do you know of, or ever work with, someone nick-named Wally? Maybe Walter someone, or someone Walters?"

Tyrell's face went blank as he thought. "No one comes to mind. There was a Jason Dell Walton that worked for us."

"Why the frown?"

"He was dismissed from the firm for making use of private client information."

"Was his work related to Maude's trust?"

"No, but I cannot guarantee that he did not look into it."

"Where is he now?"

"No idea. The police came looking for him after he left. We gave them the address we had on file for him, but he had moved from there and cleaned out his bank accounts."

"Walton," Wanda mused. "Wally?"

"What is the significance of that name?"

"I am not sure yet. What do you recall about him?"

"He was highly qualified. Had impeccable references. It was a shock to discover what he was doing. The odd thing was, I don't think anyone has heard from him since he left."

"Promising. I mentioned Wally, because Maude mentioned the name, and said, 'He from trusty place, knew face. Came to say sorry ma and pa died.'"

"My God! That rogue might be the father of the girls? Do you think it is Carson?"

"I am not going to make unfounded claims, just that Carson claims to be the father of Abbie, and she is the candidate for Gabrielle Hartley. But, I will only go as far as saying that Carson might be the father of only one of the girls."

"One? Two, surely?"

"No, actually. Have you ever heard of superfecundation?"

"No."

Wanda explained her theory, based on the DNA comparison between the two girls."

Tyrell could only shake his head. "What about the other girl?"

Wanda decided that he should know. "Do you know anyone related to the family that might be, 'Clay'?"

The colour went from Tyrell's face. "Clayton Bassenger. A close friend of both Hartley boys. For a while there was talk of him marrying Maude. He went and joined the Air Force, then married some other heiress. Though they are divorced now. So you think..."

"That anything between them was consensual."

"Did she tell you that?"

"Yes, the same way I discovered her math skill."

"I still can't really believe that, but the maths bit is a telling point. But Clayton?"

"Do you know where he is now?"

"I will see what can be done to find him. Do you think he is involved in current events?"

Wanda shrugged.

"You have given me a great deal to consider. Do you really think Maude is in danger?"

"She is safer here," Wanda told him. "I had a look over the security when I was last here. It is better than I expected."

"That's because some of the residents are apt to wander off."

"Perhaps you should suggest the cameras are monitored 24/7."

"I will do that, and be in touch."

"If you can't reach me, call David. I'm sort of on stand-down from the operational duties I was hired for, and I will be tied to a bed for about a week from tomorrow."

"Tied down?"

"That is the only way they will keep me in a hospital that

long. It's a minor op. A week is excessive."

"I will see you out," Tyrell offered.

"You're sweet, you know. But I can manage. My feet are fine."

Annie went to reception to announce herself and her friends. The receptionist knew to expect them and said the pup would be a big hit with the residents.

In fact, Maude's face lit up when she saw Annie and Lucky-pup. She smiled even wider when Naomi and Karen were introduced. She was more reserved with Baxter, even though they had already met.

Naomi's scout uniform attracted as much attention as the dog, and when Annie lifted the bag containing Maude's oddments, took Lucky Pup and pulled Karen over to introduce the dog to some of the other residents. Baxter's attention was caught by an elderly man who recognised him as a scout leader. Those two were soon talking animatedly.

Maude rummaged through the bag, and drew out items at random, telling Annie about them. She was so animated, that Annie felt a glow of pleasure.

When Baxter finally eased himself away from the old man, and caught his daughter's attention, he was struck by how many smiles were on the faces of the residents. Naomi lifted up the thoroughly spoilt Lucky-pup and went to where Annie and Maude were talking like long-time friends.

Annie looked up, and realised the time. "I'll leave the bag with you, Maude."

"No. No. You have," Maude insisted. "For me."

"You want me to look after them for you?" Annie asked for clarification. Maude nodded energetically.

"Okay, but if you want anything from it, just let me know."

"Yes, yes. Wait a bit."

Maude stood abruptly and trotted off. She returned five minutes layer with a towel wrapped bundle. "Mind too."

"Are you sure?" Annie watched as the bundle was unwrapped

and saw the baby shoes, the silver cups and the child health record books.

"Sure," Maude confirmed. "You nice, Annie. Bring Lucky again?"

"If you like," Annie agreed, with a glance at Naomi.

"Dad, it would be great to come here again. We can bring other pets to share with the residents."

"Yes, Mr Baxter. These people have so many interesting stories, I'd like to write them down," Karen added.

"Well, I will see what we can do."

Naomi put Lucky-pup down and was passing the lead to Annie when the pup decided to race off. Annie, having visions of the Friday before, ran after her. The dog was running circles around the dark haired woman who had been talking to Maude's Trustee.

"I'm sorry. She got away from me," Annie apologised, feeling her face become hot. She grabbed Lucky-pup's lead close to her collar, and carefully unwound the rest from around the woman's legs.

Without intending to, she touched the woman and was hit by a barrage of sensation – which was just as abruptly shut off.

"I'm sorry," Annie said again, when she had lifted the dog, and looked into the woman's blue eyes. It was Wanda! She was sure, but she didn't look like herself, and her arm was hurting and her ear bandaged.

"I didn't..." Annie was about to say, 'recognise you', but forced herself to stop.

"It's okay. I'm used to over excited dog."

"Wanda?" Annie whispered. A wink was the only reply.

"Are you alright?" she added, speaking a bit louder.

"Yes, thank you." The woman, so unlike Wanda in looks, turned to continue out the door.

Confused by the seeming brush off, Annie walked back to

her friends. As they were saying goodbyes, she stayed back. An idea seemed to be forming in her head. "Write everything down. Times, details, your thoughts and reasons. Send it to Kelly. Or to David to send on."

Yes. Kelly had quizzed her, but not asked for a statement. Annie tried a test, "Will it help Martin?"

All of a sudden, she wanted to grin like an idiot, feeling sure she was right. She buried her head in Lucky's coat until the sensation went away. Then she tried to recall what she had sensed from Wanda, but it was like she had never felt it. If only she could control her own mind that well. Then she realised that the feeling of pique at the brush off had gone too. She had been privileged to receive a thought sent telepathically.

She hoped that someone would tell her what was going on, but this time, she felt no response.

"What are you grinning at?" Naomi asked her.

"What? Oh! I just feel so good. Did you see all the smiles?" It wasn't the full truth, but it would serve.

"Yes. These people can't get visitors very often. Poor things. I am going to keep pushing Dad to let us come back."

"I'd come even without doing it for scouts," Karen agreed. "Next time, I'm going to bring a voice recorder and record the stories."

Annie used the excuse of taking Lucky-pup for a walk to head to the shop. She hoped to find Martin there, at work. She had obeyed David's request not to try contacting him, even though he had given no reason. Coming to the shop wasn't doing that – not exactly.

At the door, she lifted Lucky-pup up. The shopkeeper's eyes lit up seeing them. He came to make a fuss of the little dog. "Mr Cato, has Martin been in?"

The man's expression changed and he shook his head. "He

hasn't rung me."

Annie hid her face in Lucky's fur for a moment, wondering if she should tell him what she knew. She was about to speak when an unwelcome voice stopped her.

"The little cuz got himself locked up," Tom Logan sneered.

"You'd best find a new boyfriend, Jamieson," Gerry added.

Annie didn't turn around, asking instead, "Would I be able to have a copy of the Women's Weekly, please."

The Logans persisted in their derogatory comments as Cato turned to reach for the magazine. The bell at the door announced another customer, and Cato nodded a greeting.

"Are you listening, Jamieson? He was caught with a case full of drugs," Tom Logan persisted.

Annie turned, and forced herself to act casually. "Since you know all about it, it must mean you set him up again."

"Hey! He's the one that keeps trying to get us in trouble," Gerry protested.

"Oh, I don't know. You both manage that quite well by yourselves."

Tom moved closer but stopped when Lucky-pup growled. "They had cops at his place again yesterday, searching the place."

"And was that where that mythical case of drugs was found?"

"You think I'm lying, Jamieson?" Tom challenged. "The cuz is locked up right now, in Melbourne."

"He's a pathetic loser," Gerry added. "Like you will be if you don't ditch him."

"You're pathetic," Annie told them, then turned to pay for the magazine.

Tom was reaching out to swing her around, when his wrist was grabbed. "What the –"

Annie caught the look on Gerry's face. Whoever the man was, it was obvious he was not someone they wanted to see.

Annie caught sight of another figure behind the man facing the Logans. She recognised him, but when he simply shook his head at her, she said nothing. Instead, she noticed how his whole bearing changed as if he was about to play a role.

"Tom and Gerald Logan," he stated. His words drew the attention of both boys. The first man seemed startled at first, then a faint grin appeared on his face.

"I'm David Davis of the Atlas Task Force."

The Logans looked blankly at him. "I am assisting the local police with several investigations. I overheard your comment about your cousin and would very much like to discuss what you know."

"Ah, we don't know anything, really," Gerry protested immediately.

"No, we were just making it up," Tom supported his brother.

"The ideas must have come from somewhere," David suggested. He decided to twist the truth a little. "I am aware that a drug exchange was to take place. Are you sure it was the police who picked up your cousin?"

Neither Tom nor Gerry seemed to know what to say now. David went on, "I will admit that I wasn't coming here to talk to you, but I am glad I caught you. I know you are both friends of Tory Michaelson, and I think it will be profitable to talk to both of you down at the local police station."

While still watching both Logans, David reached for his phone and flipped it open. He dialled a number by feel.

"Kelly? It's David. I would like to bring two young men to the station for questions...yes, thank you."

The other man, his face again stern, asked, "Should I call their father and arrange a lawyer?"

"You are welcome to accompany them, and if you feel there

is a need, to arrange a lawyer. My questions are simple, and if they choose to answer, I won't be insisting on any charges. It is obvious they don't care about their kinfolk, I expect they don't care about friends or other people either."

"What do you want to know?" Tom blurted, urgently.

"This is not the place for it," David stated implacably.

Five minutes later, an unmarked police car pulled up. Kelly emerged and strode into the shop. David gave him a terse greeting and casually mentioned the claim that had caught his attention. Kelly's expression grew harder as he shared the idea that had occurred to the American. Someone knew what had happened to Martin when the matter had been carefully kept from outsiders.

"I will follow with their uncle, shortly," David told him.

The two now cowed twins walked in front of Kelly to the police car, and the other detective gestured them into the car.

"Is Martin really okay?" Annie dared to ask once the boys were out of the shop.

"Yes," David assured her. "I can't discuss it, but he should be back home either today or tomorrow. I will let him tell as much or as little as he wants. Please don't discuss anything he says with anyone else."

"I won't," Annie promised.

David turned to the shopkeeper. "You would be Mr Cato?"

The man nodded.

"Martin has passed on an apology for not being able to help you yesterday or today. He will be available later in the week."

"Is he in trouble? Can I help? He is a good boy," Cato said, each sentence coming out fast.

"I know," David agreed. "Yes, he's in trouble, but it wasn't his choice. I have made sure he has legal representation, and he should be able to be released on bail."

"I can pay for the lawyer," Cato offered.

David smiled. "That has been taken care of. What I know Martin will appreciate is that his job with you is still here for him."

"Yes, yes. Tell him I keep job for him."

"Thank you," David said, nodding goodbye.

The man waiting nearby murmured to David. "I will see to the bail."

Annie followed David to the door. "David? What happened to Wanda? Is she in trouble too?"

"Trouble? No more than normal." David's grin seemed forced. In a lower voice, he said, "She's being a decoy. Playing a role."

"Oh. That's dangerous?"

"It can be. I can't say more about it. I hope you understand."

"I guess," Annie agreed. "But she's been hurt."

"Most of that was from Friday morning," David said. He had recognised Eduardo, Martin's uncle, and didn't want him to know part of the story. "And she didn't exactly stop using her injured arm after that. She is going in for an operation tomorrow."

"Can we visit her?" Annie asked.

David's grin was easier when he said, "I will have to see if it's okay, and make sure she hasn't discharged herself first. I will let you know and I will let her know of your concern."

Annie thanked him, and put Lucky-pup down for the walk home. The poor little dog hadn't wriggled much at all, a sign she was tired. She, however, felt happier and energised. Martin was okay. David was on his side. Wanda would be okay too. That reminded her of Wanda's suggestion of writing down all that had happened the previous day. She'd do that first thing after tea.

David offered Eduardo a lift, and the man accepted. "So, Wanda's uncles took off, did they?"

Eduardo chuckled. "With Interpol breathing down their

necks, I understand.”

David just shook his head and changed the subject. “Are you watching those two now?”

“Yes.”

“Have you any idea how they found out about their cousin? Does Nikolai know about it?”

“Nicholas is aware of the matter, and he is vehemently against people who deal in drugs. However, those step sons of his would not have learnt of it from him.”

“Is Kemple into that?”

“He is an opportunist,” Eduardo’s tone was vicious. “And he is a coward. Do you think those boys know where he is?”

“I am hoping they do. He is a loose end, I want tied up.”

“If they don’t know, I will help you find him. My sister is upset that her son is accused of such a nasty crime.”

“Is there a reason why your kin have cut him off?”

“We do as told. I think you must have some inkling. However, if you know about us, do you think he is better left as a stranger?”

David gave a low chuckle. “Yes.”

“I would wish my other nephews had his determination and sense. Instead they idle their time away. My brother-in-law has thought to send them to our foreign relatives, who may be able to teach them their place and to apply themselves to a worthwhile career.”

Asking what that might be, David decided, would not be a tactful idea. He wanted to keep Martin’s uncle on his side.

Eduardo went on. “Maybe you can scare some sense into them. Make them realise that they do not lead a charmed life.”

“I will try to sound like a bigger predator than they think themselves.”

Eduardo chuckled. “Bigger than your mate? Do send her my regards for a speedy recovery too. I did enjoy seeing her stand up to Leo.”

<u>Chapter 6</u>

Wanda went back to Kelso's house where she and David were spending most of their time. She needed to remove the dark colour from her hair, and the rest of her disguise. She hadn't wanted Maude to know she was at the community house that time, but it had been the perfect place for her and Tyrell to talk.

She was disappointed to find that David had gone out, and surprised to see Commander Britten there. His reaction to seeing her disguise did amuse her.

"Commander. Were you waiting to see me?"

"Yes. I wanted to see how you were. I had a report from the doctor."

Wanda grimaced. The diagnosis had not pleased her at all. "He said he knew an excellent specialist and an operation should fix me up as good as new. I had hoped for better than new, though."

Britten smiled faintly. "I have organised for all of your medical costs here to be covered."

"Thank you, Sir."

"Now, official matters. The Task Force is in the process of changing base. The passive tracer on that envelope suggests it is on a plane heading towards Europe. As a result, the local police who have been working with us have been detached from the Task Force, but are on notice that they may be reattached if required."

"And David and I?" Wanda asked. "Are we being dumped?"

"On the contrary. You, however, need time out to recover. So, while currently on stand down, you and David may be reactivated in the future as well."

"I understand," Wanda said, so he would know she was in agreement.

"I am also going to recommend you and David for an official commendation. You may not get a fancy certificate, but I am aware that you both provided service beyond expectations."

"So, you will want our ID tags?" Wanda expected him to say 'yes'.

"Normally, yes, but I have been hearing more about what Kelso hopes you can do for him. I am impressed that you found time to help less able people. For now, keep the ID, but once you leave Australia to go home, I expect both IDs to be returned to HQ in Washington."

"Yes, Sir."

"That way, I will know who to second in future."

Wanda grinned. "I thought you didn't like mavericks."

"Only unprincipled ones."

"Wow! I really put one over you, didn't I?"

Britten held out his hand to shake her free one. Then with a nod, he turned and went out to the car Wanda had seen parked outside.

David arrived back at Kelso's place fairly satisfied with his day's work. Putting a scare into Martin's cousins had indeed yielded the location of Kevin Kemple. He had been celebrating his son's disgrace when Kelly and Kaspersky had walked into the bar of the Regal Hotel in Footscray. He had heard the news through the criminal grapevine. One of his mates had been picked up and taken to the city and had been in a position to hear the charge against Martin. The Logans had heard it from Tory Michaelson, now out on bail.

As he locked the car, he checked the time and realised that Wanda would need to return to the hospital soon. He hurried inside.

Wanda had reached him even before he'd finished closing the door. He was happy to enfold her in a hug, while being careful of her sore arm.

"Get a room, you two," Thea commented from one of the chairs.

Wanda eased away and said, "What kept you? You missed on of Kelso's famous stir frys."

"I'll eat later. You ready?"

"No," Wanda growled, even though there was a packed back pack by the door.

"I see you got the black dye out okay," David commented.

"Thea helped me, since you weren't around. What's the latest?"

"Kemple has been picked up," David said with satisfaction, and then related the Logan brothers' ordeal. "Oh and your friend Eduardo wishes you well."

"Abbie's home safely?"

"She should be by now. Though I think Carson needs to tone down his attitude. I put a listening device in his house and it is still sending. I heard enough of his tirade when I was copying it from my phone to the computer. Do you want me to take you to the hospital?"

"Of course I do!"

Kelso called form his office, "David, do you have a few minutes?"

Wanda released him, reluctantly. She had an idea what Kelso wanted him for, but she was to have no active role in anything until she was out of the hospital. She already knew that Fred was to drop her off, but, she had hoped.

Tyrell came to visit Kelso later that evening, hoping to speak to Wanda again. David, who had been getting to know Thea, excused himself to talk to him.

"She had to go back to the hospital. She's going to have an operation tomorrow morning," he explained.

"Oh! Maude was asking if she could be present when I met with Mr Carson."

"Will she be there?" David asked. "Has she remembered him?"

"No. I advised her to wait until we were sure. Now that the girl has been found, we can reschedule the meeting. Maude trusts Wanda's impressions of things."

Kelso let David respond to that. "Right now, I don't think Wanda needs to be in the same room as Jeremy Carson. She's encountered him whilst doing his background check."

"I understand," Tyrell nodded. "She mentioned some of her concerns earlier, when I spoke to her. Give her my best wishes for a speedy recovery, will you?"

David nodded and went to see Tyrell out.

Thea, a silent listener to the exchange, finally spoke up. "My brother has some pictures of our father, from when we were little. He didn't have black hair then."

"Do you think," Kelso commented, carefully neutral, as he came to sit in a chair near Thea, "that he will permit us to have a look?"

Thea shrank back into her chair. "Maybe. Do you think he's a crook? Carson, I mean."

Kelso worded his answer carefully. "If he is, we want to know."

"Wanda had five minutes with Robbo, earlier today," David told Thea. "He wasn't volunteering anything, but he may have been a bit out of it still. She asked him if he knew of two names, one he did and one he didn't. That name had cropped up in another investigation."

All of a sudden, Thea looked more like the confident 'punk' David had seen in the security footage from the local school. As he walked over to put the Foxtel news channel on, he decided that Thea considered that information as confirmation of her belief about Carson. He hoped that they would agree to share what had made them sure Carson was their father.

In the meantime, he wanted to look over the news reports of the happy reunion with Abbie and her parents as they left the hospital. He also wanted to watch Thea's reactions.

The story continues in Volume 4.

**Touching Other Lives
Volume 4**
Episode 22: Annie Gets in Trouble
Episode 23: Hostile Intentions
Episode 24: Not So Clever
Episode 25: Closing in
Episode 26: Change of Luck
Episode 27: Upside Down

Also by Margaret Gregory

<u>TYMOREAN TRUST SERIES: (Fantasy)</u>
Book 1 - Power Rising
Book 2 - Great Ones
Book 3 - The Return to Earth
Book 4 – Earth Mission
Book 5 – Alien Contact
Book 6 - Invasion

<u>ATAPI SORCERESS SERIES: (Fantasy)</u>
Prequel – Korvu: The Beginning
Book 1- The Wild One
Book 2 – Atapi Sorceress

<u>THE THIRD GENERATION SERIES:(Fantasy)</u>
Book 1 - Wanda: From Bad to Worse
Book 2 - Wanda: Choosing Crime
Wanda – Early Days (anthology) Book 1 and 2
Book 3 – Wanda: Risking Life to Live
Book 4 – Erin: The Forcing of Wisdom
Book 5 – Wanda: A New Life Part 1 – Hidden Secrets
Book 6 – Wanda: A New Life Part 2 – First Mission
Book 7 – Wanda: Full Circle
The Serpent's Shadow
Royal Favour
Foreign Agent - Thief
Prisoner - Spy

<u>HOLDER OF SECRETS SERIES:</u>
Unregarded
Unsuspected
Unrepentant

<u>STAND ALONE</u>
The Magpie's Daughter
The Chance to be Me
Maeven: Dragon Thief